THE LOPSIDED
CHRISTMAS
CAKE

THE LOPSIDED
CHRISTMAS
CAKE

WANDA E. BRUNSTETTER

& JEAN BRUNSTETTER

BARBOUR BOOKS
An Imprint of Barbour Publishing, Inc.

Dedication

To our husbands, Richard Sr. and Richard Jr.
We appreciate your love and support.
A special thanks to Mary Alice Yoder for
your friendship and helpfulness.

*He that handleth a matter wisely shall find good:
and whoso trusteth in the Lord, happy is he.*
PROVERBS 16:20

Prologue

Elma Hochstetler sat quietly beside her twin sister, Thelma, as their somber father read his parents' will. He'd found it last week after the funeral but had waited until now to read it to them.

Dad leaned forward, looking right at the twins. "Girls, it appears that you two have inherited my folks' house, as well as their store."

The twins gasped in unison.

"Once your *daed* has talked to a lawyer and the paperwork has been finalized, you can sell both places," Mom interjected.

Dad touched Mom's arm. "Kathryn, I think this is something we ought to let the girls decide."

Tears threatened to spill from Elma's eyes as she allowed Dad's words to sink in. It had been difficult to accept that her grandparents had been killed when their horse and buggy were hit by a truck. Hearing this news was an even greater shock. Elma had assumed that Dad, being their only son, would inherit their estate. Why would Grandma and Grandpa want her and Thelma to have it?

Full of questions, Elma squeezed her sister's hand. "What do you think we should do about this?"

Tears glistened in Thelma's blue eyes. She drew in a quick breath. "If Grandma and Grandpa wanted us to have their house and store, I think we should honor their wishes."

"But you can't move all the way to Indiana. We rely on you both to help at our store here." Mom's forehead wrinkled. "Besides, your grandparents didn't run things the way we do."

"You worry too much, Kathryn." Dad removed his glasses. "We'll hire a couple of girls to work in our store. The twins can run my folks' business however they want." He looked at Elma and Thelma. "In fact, I think you ought to go there as soon as possible."

Mom's brown eyes widened. "Why, Jacob? What's the rush? This is a big decision."

"It's not good to leave my parents' house sitting empty too long. And my folks' store needs to be up and running again. Their community relies on it." Dad rose to his feet. "I'm going out to the phone shack and call one of our drivers. Thelma and Elma, you need to get packed."

Drying her tears, Thelma smiled. "This could be an adventure. I don't know about you, Elma, but it feels right to me."

Elma nodded slowly, although she felt overwhelmed. Looking around their parents' living room, a lump formed in her throat. This was the only home she and her sister had ever known. Taking over their grandparents' place in Topeka meant she and Thelma would have to move three hundred miles away. Fortunately, they had experience running a store, since they'd been helping at their parents' general store from the time they were girls. But they weren't girls anymore. Although they looked much younger, Elma and Thelma had turned thirty-two last month. They still lived at home, and neither of them was married or even had a serious boyfriend. There really was nothing keeping them here. The question was, would they be able to take on such a monumental task by themselves?

Chapter 1

Standing in the front yard, while gazing at their grandparents' rambling old two-story house, all Elma Hochstetler could do was shake her head in disbelief. Glancing toward the road as their driver disappeared, Elma bit her lip. *This is it. There's no going back.*

Overcome with emotion, she turned to face Thelma. "I can't believe this place is really ours."

Holding the orange-and-white cat that had sauntered up to them, Thelma nodded.

Everything from the weeds choking out the garden to the sagging front porch and peeling paint spoke of one thing—work. The barn and other outbuildings were run-down too. Since this was the first week of September, Elma knew they would have to get some of the outside chores done before the harsh winter set in.

How quiet it was. She hadn't noticed that before when they'd visited Grandpa and Grandma. Their grandparents' home was on a side road, with farms on both sides of it. The home across the street had a For Sale sign out front.

As they stepped onto the porch, Thelma paused and tipped her head. "Listen to the tinkle of Grandma's wind chimes."

Barely noticing the chimes, Elma pointed to the eaves above the porch. "Oh my. There's an ugly brown spider up there."

"It's nothing to worry about. I'll take care of it later." Thelma stroked the cat's head. "I think it'll be fun to fix this place up."

Elma shook her head. "Fun? You think all the effort it will take to get this place livable is going to be fun? I'd call it work. And some of it will take money we don't have."

"You're right, but we can have fun in the process." Thelma's exuberance was almost contagious. But then, even when the twins were children Thelma hadn't worried about things. "Free-spirited." That's what Dad called Thelma, while he'd labeled Elma as "the serious one." While the physically identical twins shared the same petite frame, blue eyes, and chestnut brown hair, their personalities didn't always mesh.

I suppose I am too serious, Elma thought ruefully. *But someone has to stay focused. It takes organization to keep things running smoothly. If I followed my twin sister's path, we'd spend every day looking through rose-colored glasses.*

Thelma released the cat and slipped her arm around Elma's waist. "We've always done everything together, right?"

Elma could only nod, watching a clump of cat hair float through the air.

"Together, we'll turn this place back into what it used to be before Grandma and Grandpa got too old to keep everything up."

Thelma smiled. "We'll make this a *glicklich* adventure."

Elma knew her sister had good intentions and was thinking positively. Even though the situation looked overwhelming, perhaps Thelma was right. "*Jah,* we'll make it successful," Elma said. "The first thing we should do is go grocery shopping, because I'm sure there's not much fresh food in Grandma's kitchen."

"I think we should've accepted Mom's offer to help us organize this place," Thelma said as she mopped the kitchen floor the following day.

"This is *our* project." After disposing of some out-of-date canned fruit and vegetables they'd found in a cupboard, Elma placed the empty jars in the sink. "Besides, Mom has plenty to do at home, taking care of the house and helping

Dad at the store. They'll be coming here in a few weeks to visit. I want to surprise them with all we've gotten done."

Thelma grimaced. "They'll be surprised all right. Mom will wonder why we don't sell this place and move back home."

"Hey, where's that positive attitude you had yesterday? This is our home now," Elma reminded. "Grandma and Grandpa's store is our only source of income." She opened another jar and dumped the contents into the garbage can. "Can you believe all the green beans Grandma canned two summers ago? It's a shame to waste all this food."

"It is a waste, but it's not safe to eat something that old." Thelma plugged her nose. "Smell that musty odor?" She drew the curtain aside that hid the items under the sink. "Uh-oh. It looks like the pipe's been leaking for some time. Grandma must have tied this old thin rag around it to stifle the dripping. Eww...it's soaking wet." Thelma rubbed her hands over her apron and pointed to something else. "There's a coffee can under the pipe to catch the water. It's nearly full."

"You'd better dump it. We should get that fixed as soon as possible, but for now we should find a thicker piece of material to secure around the leak." Elma pushed her dress sleeves up. "I've started a list of things that need to be done. It would be good if you started a list too in case I miss anything."

Thelma scrunched her nose. "Oh no. Not more lists!"

"They do help when there's so much to be done."

"I suppose. One thing I know we need to do is paint." Thelma gestured to the wall behind the woodstove. It was coated with soot.

"You're right," Elma agreed. "I think most of the rooms in this house could use some paint. That alone will help to spruce things up."

Thelma pushed a piece of her hair back under the black scarf covering her bun. Then she gestured to the missing handles on a few of the cupboard doors. "The whole place seems to be falling apart. Didn't Grandpa fix anything?"

"He and Grandma were old. Their health was slipping before the accident." Elma spoke in a quieter tone, tears welling in her eyes. "I think it was too much for him to keep up."

"You're probably right," Thelma agreed, "but wouldn't you think they would have sold the place and moved to Sullivan to be closer to family?"

"Remember, Dad tried to talk them into moving." Elma rinsed another jar. "But our grandparents were too independent to budge. They would probably still be running their store if the accident hadn't happened. Besides, it can't be easy selling the home you've always known." Tears clung to her lashes. She would miss seeing them. Grandpa told funny jokes. Grandma knew how to cook better than anyone and always had a delicious treat waiting whenever the twins came to visit.

Unfortunately, due to how busy they'd been at their folks' store, the twins hadn't made a trip to see their grandparents for two years. That saddened Elma, because she and Thelma hadn't been able to see Grandma and Grandpa before they'd died. But knowing they'd been entrusted with this old house and the store fueled her determination to make a go of it.

"Guess I can't blame Grandma and Grandpa for staying put," Thelma admitted. "This place was special to them. It was their home for as long as I can remember." She pushed the mop under the table. "It's hard for older people to lose their independence and rely on others." She sighed. "I don't look forward to getting old."

"Try not to worry about aging," Elma said. "Let's take one day at a time and try to—"

"Enjoy the moments we have on earth." Thelma finished her sister's sentence and set the mop aside. "I don't know about you, but I'm tired of working. With all the organizing and decluttering, we'll never find time to do anything fun."

Elma flapped her hand. "Oh, sure we will. The holidays will be coming soon. There'll be all sorts of fun things to do."

"Like what?"

"We can go Christmas caroling. If we get enough

snow, we can get that old sleigh out of Grandpa's barn."

Thelma perked up. "A sleigh ride sounds fun. We can put bells on the horse's harness, and sing Christmas songs, like Grandpa used to do when we were little."

"Don't forget the holiday baking we'll get to do," Elma put in. "We can make Grandma's special Christmas cake—you know, the one she used to fix whenever we came to visit during the holidays."

"I've always liked that special cake with Jell-O in it." Thelma gestured to the woodstove across the room. "If we have to use that old relic, everything we make will probably flop. Besides, I'm not the world's best baker."

"We can't afford to buy a propane-operated stove right now. We'll make the best of what we have." Elma had removed another jar from the cupboard when she spotted a little gray mouse skittering across the floor. Startled, she loosened her grip on the jar, sending it crashing to the floor. "*Ach!* Did you see that?"

"See what?"

Elma dashed into the utility room, grabbing the broom. Instead of cleaning the mess, she shoved it under the stove, swishing it back and forth.

"What are you doing, and what did you see?"

"There's a *maus* in here! Didn't you see it?"

"No, I didn't, and you won't get it with that. We need to bring in one of the *katze*. Grandpa always said his cats were good mousers."

Elma grimaced. "You know I don't like katze in the house."

"Would you rather have a maus?"

Elma shook her head vigorously. "They're *ekelhaft* little creatures."

"If you think they're disgusting, then let me bring in a cat."

"Okay." Elma grabbed a dustpan. She swept up the broken glass and beans. "After he gets the maus, make sure he goes outside."

13

When Thelma stepped outside, she spotted one of the cats curled in a ball on the saggy porch. "Come with me, Tiger." She bent down and picked up the cat. "You have a job to do in the kitchen. I'll bet you'll appreciate the meal." Even though one of the neighbors had been feeding the animals since her grandparents had died, this cat looked scrawny.

Meow! Tiger opened his eyes, looking at Thelma as if to say, "Why'd you wake me?"

Thelma took the cat inside and set him on the floor near the stove. "Get the mouse, boy!"

Elma's gaze went to the ceiling. "You think he's gonna listen to you?"

"Tiger may not understand what I said, but if that mouse moves, the cat will spring into action." Thelma stood back with her arms folded, waiting to see what would happen.

"Tiger?"

"Jah. That's what I named him because of his color. I think it fits. Don't you?"

"I guess so."

Tiger sat a few seconds then turned toward a moth that had flown into the room. Thelma ducked. She'd never cared much for moths, especially when they flew toward her face. Tiger took off in good form, heading for his prey that now hovered over the bucket of ashes near the stove. The cat leaped into the air and upset the container.

"*Die katz laaft im esch!*" Elma shouted.

Thelma groaned. Her sister was right—Tiger walked in the cinders and had caught his airborne snack. She knew if she didn't get him quick, he'd be tracking the mess all over her clean floor.

Thelma dashed across the room, but when she was about to grab the cat, the mouse shot out from under the stove. Elma shrieked and jumped on a chair. Dropping the moth, Tiger chased the mouse. Thelma raced for the door.

Jerking it open, she was relieved when the mouse made its escape. Tiger followed. Slamming the door, she turned to face her sister. "You can come down now. It's safe."

"For now, anyway," Elma muttered, stepping down from the chair. "If there's one *maus* in the house, there's bound to be more. What if there's a whole family of them?"

"Maybe I should bring Tiger back in," Thelma suggested.

Elma shook her head. "Not now. I think we've done enough here this morning. Let's finish cleaning this mess. Then we can fix lunch. When we're done eating, we can head over to the store to see what needs to be done there."

When they'd finished cleaning the floor, Elma stepped out of the room and came back with a notebook. "Here's the list I started. I'll make another one when we go out to the store."

"Pretty soon we'll have so many lists you won't know which one to look at," Thelma teased; then she got serious. "Do you think we should hire someone to help us in the store? That would give us more time to do some other things around here."

Elma shook her head. "Maybe later. Right now we can't afford to hire anyone." She opened the refrigerator, glad they'd had time yesterday to pick up a few things at the grocery store. "What kind of sandwich would you like—ham or bologna?"

Thelma shrugged. "I don't care. You choose."

Elma took out the packages of lunch meat. "I'm hungry enough to eat two sandwiches, so let's have both."

"Sounds good to me." Thelma got out the bread.

Elma placed the lunch meat on the counter and opened the packages. "You know, Thelma, I've been thinking that it's good for us to be on our own. After all, we're not *kinner* anymore. We need to prove to ourselves, and also to Mom and Dad, that we can make a go of things."

"You're right." Thelma gave Elma's arm a tender squeeze. "With the Lord's help, we can handle most anything."

Chapter 2

I wonder if we'll ever get this yard in shape." Elma kicked some scattered leaves as they walked past a dead bush. "There's so much to do here; I feel overwhelmed by it all."

Thelma clasped her sister's arm. "Don't worry so much. It'll get done in good time."

"I hope so, but that's our first priority." Elma motioned to the general store, several feet behind the house. According to Grandpa, with the help of his friends, he built the store a few years after he and Grandma were married.

When Thelma heard chickens clucking, she glanced to the left. "I just remembered, we didn't check for eggs last night. Think I'd better do that right now."

"Go ahead. I'll head over to the store and start organizing some of the shelves." Elma took a few steps in that direction but turned around. "Don't be long. There's lots of work, and it's going to take both of us."

"Don't worry. It won't take much time to gather a few eggs. I'll join you shortly."

After Elma walked away, Thelma headed for the chicken coop. *My sister worries too much. People shopped at Grandpa and Grandma's store when it wasn't perfectly organized. If we don't have everything just so, I'm sure it won't affect our business.*

Thelma thought about her folks' store back home and how, between Mom and Elma, everything was kept neat and tidy. One or both of them seemed to be constantly cleaning and organizing. Thelma had never enjoyed cleaning that much. Organizing was definitely not her thing.

She'd rather wait on customers so she could visit.

When Thelma opened the door to the coop, she was greeted by several cackling hens. She remembered collecting eggs with Grandpa when she was a little girl. He would talk about a few of his favorite chickens and had even given them names.

Thelma fed the chickens first and gave them fresh water. When that was done, she grabbed a basket and filled it with eggs. It was fun to see the different colors. Not all the chickens were the same, and not all of the eggs were white. Some hens laid eggs in various colors. She was surprised to see any eggs at all, since one of Grandma's neighbors had been taking care of the animals. Perhaps, since they knew Thelma and Elma would arrive yesterday, they hadn't collected any more eggs.

Thelma hummed, reaching under a stubborn hen that wouldn't move off its nest. *Bawk! Bawk!* The chicken ruffled her feathers and hopped to the floor, looking back at Thelma as if to say, "How dare you steal my egg."

Thelma looked out the small window facing the corral. She saw Rusty, the horse Grandpa bought a few months before he died. His old horse, Cutter, had been pulling their rig the day of the accident and was killed. That left only Rusty available to the twins. Unfortunately, he was still a bit green and would be a challenge. *One more problem,* she thought.

Satisfied that she'd gotten all the eggs, Thelma moved toward the door. "Oh great," she chided herself when she realized that she'd left it open. "Sure hope none of the chickens got out."

Thelma's brows furrowed as she stepped outside and saw chickens roaming all over the yard. "Good grief! Now I have chickens to round up."

She set the basket on the ground and moved toward the nearest chicken. Apparently, the hen didn't want to be caught, because it took off like a flash. The other chickens scattered too.

The chickens really didn't need to be in the coop all

day. She'd wait until nightfall, when they would be subject to predators, to put the birds back in their coop. They'd be easier to catch when it started getting dark, and she'd have Elma's help.

Thelma grabbed the basket and hurried into the house. She took care of the eggs first then paused for a drink of water. After working in the kitchen most of the morning, Thelma was tired. Too bad Elma wanted to work at the store right now. Thelma wanted to sit outside and work on the gloves she'd begun knitting for Mom's Christmas gift.

Maybe I'll get my knitting out now and do a couple of rows, she decided. *If I sit a few minutes, I'll have more energy to help Elma clean the store.*

Elma swiped a trickle of sweat on her forehead and pushed a wayward hair under her scarf. If the store had been open for business today she would have worn her stiff white head covering. But with all the sweeping and dusting she'd been doing, her normal covering would have gotten dirty.

Elma glanced at the battery-operated clocks near the door. She'd been in the store over an hour already. Where was Thelma?

"She probably got distracted, like she often does," Elma mumbled. "Guess I'd better find her." She set her broom aside and hurried from the store, leaving the door open to air the place out. Glancing toward the chicken coop, she noticed the door was open. Surely, Thelma couldn't still be gathering eggs.

Elma stepped into the coop. No sign of her sister there—only a couple of hens on their nests. *Thelma must be in the house. Doing what, I can't imagine.*

When Elma entered the house, she was surprised to see Thelma sitting in Grandma's rocking chair, clicking away with her knitting needles.

"What are you doing?" Elma stepped in front of Thelma.

Thelma blinked rapidly, her cheeks turning pink.

"I—I was tired and sat down with my knitting to relax a few minutes."

Elma's hands went straight to her hips. "I thought you were coming out to the store to help me. If we don't get the place cleaned and organized, we'll never be ready to open for business."

"I know, and I'm sorry. I lost track of time."

"I don't see how this is going to work if you get distracted so easily and leave me to manage things by myself."

"I'll try to do better." Thelma set her knitting aside. "Let's head to the store."

Elma opened the door and squealed when Tiger brushed her ankles as he darted into the house. "Oh great, now we have a katz to catch."

"Let's leave him here while we're at the store," Thelma suggested. "If there's another maus, he might catch it and we won't have to worry about setting any traps."

Elma shook her head. "We can't leave the cat in the house unattended. After what he did earlier, who knows what kind of mess he could make. Besides, he's shedding. I don't want cat hair in the house."

"I could stay and catch the cat."

"Oh sure, and leave me to do all the work? No way! We'll both try to capture the cat."

Elma and Thelma went through the house, calling for Tiger, but he seemed to have disappeared.

"Now what?" Elma frowned.

Thelma shrugged. "Tiger's bound to come out sometime. He can't stay hidden forever. I suppose we could stay here and work in the store later."

"The longer we put that off, the longer it'll be till we can hang the OPEN sign in the front window." Elma released a frustrated sigh. "As much as I dislike the idea, I think we'd better leave the cat in the house. Hopefully, he's found a place to sleep and won't wake up for a while."

"If that's what you want to do." Thelma turned toward the door. "I promise, the first chance I get I'll look for a brush and go over his coat real good. And don't worry, I'll do that outside."

Elma followed her, making sure to close the door. The last thing they needed was another cat getting in—or a bunch of chickens.

As they neared the store, Elma halted. "Look, Thelma, there are two horse and buggies at the hitching rail."

"Oh good, we have company!" Thelma grinned. "Maybe some of our neighbors have come to get acquainted."

Elma groaned. "More than likely we have customers who think the store is open. This is not what we needed today, Sister."

Chapter 3

When Thelma entered the store, she was excited to see four women and five young children. She recognized Sadie Yoder from Grandma and Grandpa's funeral. Perhaps she'd met the other women too, but the day of the funeral had been such a blur. She'd been introduced to so many people she couldn't remember them all.

"Hello, everyone." Thelma smiled, and her voice grew louder. "It's nice to see you." She glanced at Elma and noticed that her smile appeared to be forced. Wasn't she happy to see all these people?

"As soon as we saw the store's open door, we figured you were open." Sadie held a cardboard box. "When we heard you were coming, we decided to bring you some food. It's our way of welcoming you to the area."

"That's right," another woman, who introduced herself as Doris Miller, spoke up. "Mine is still in my buggy, and so are the boxes Clara Lehman and Mary Lambright brought." She gestured to the other two friends. One of them had two small boys with her, and the other had two girls and a boy. The children all appeared to be under the age of six, which meant they hadn't started school yet.

Looking at their cute little faces, Thelma couldn't help feeling a bit envious. She loved children and longed to be a wife and mother, but as the years slipped by, she'd begun to lose hope. She'd had a few suitors, and so had Elma, but none of the men had seemed quite right for them. And they'd never been courted at the same time. Thelma

21

WANDA $\mathcal{E}$. BRUNSTETTER & JEAN BRUNSTETTER

still remembered as a little girl promising her sister that she would never get married unless Elma was getting married too.

Glancing back at her sister, Thelma was relieved to see Elma's relaxed expression. "*Danki.* That's so kind of you," Elma said. "If you'd like to bring your food items to the house, I'll get them put away."

"That's fine," Sadie replied. "We'll see that everything is taken in." She and Doris followed Elma outside, but the other two women and their children remained in the store. Thelma wondered if they wanted to visit or planned to do some shopping. She hoped that wasn't the case, because Elma had made it clear this morning that they wouldn't open until the cleaning and organizing was done.

Thelma turned to Clara and asked, "Do you live nearby?"

Clara shook her head. "Our home is several miles away. Having three little ones, I don't make trips to the store as often as I'd like." She glanced toward the stacked material. "I need some fabric. Is it all right if my kinner look at your children's books while I choose the cloth?"

Thelma nodded. What else could she do? It wouldn't be right to turn the woman down.

"Do you still carry vitamins here?" Mary asked.

"Umm. . .I'm not sure. We haven't had a chance to take inventory yet, but you're welcome to look around."

"I'll do that." Mary motioned to her boys. "Is it okay if Philip and Richard look at the children's books too?"

"That's fine with me," Thelma replied. "In fact, I'll take a book off the shelf and read them a story."

As Mary and Clara started shopping, Thelma placed a braided throw rug on the floor. After the children took a seat, she found an appropriate book and sat beside them. "Solomon Lapp was a very smart boy," she began reading in Pennsylvania Dutch, so the children would understand. "He always got the best grades in school. He fed the cows faster than his five brothers. He gathered eggs quicker than his three sisters."

The children giggled when Thelma showed them a picture of Solomon riding his scooter. She loved to see them enjoying the story and wished she could sit with these sweet children the rest of the day.

"You can set the boxes on the table," Elma said when she entered the kitchen with Sadie and Doris. "Again, it was so thoughtful of you to think of me and my sister this way."

Sadie, the older woman, touched Elma's arm. "We were all saddened when your grandparents passed away, but we're glad you and your sister have taken over their place." Her hazel eyes clouded, and she wiped a tear that had dribbled down her cheek.

"Jah," Doris agreed. "We are so glad you're here." She pushed her metal-framed glasses back in place. "I didn't know your grandparents as well as some of the others, because my husband and I are new to the area. But from what we've heard, they were both a blessing to this community."

Elma's throat tightened. She had to fight to control her emotions. The kind things these women said about Grandma and Grandpa made her miss them even more.

Refocusing her thoughts, she unloaded the boxes. They held everything from home-canned fruits and vegetables to casserole dishes, packages of meat, and several kinds of desserts.

Sadie passed Elma another item. "If there's anything we can help you with, please don't hesitate to ask."

"Danki," Elma said. "We'll let you know if we need any help."

She had put the last item in the refrigerator, when Tiger darted into the room—chasing a mouse of all things. *Oh no, not now!* Not wanting to embarrass herself, Elma fought the urge to scream and hop onto a chair.

As though this was an everyday occurrence, Doris

chuckled. "Would you look at that?"

Sadie laughed too, and Elma sighed with relief. Either these ladies were very kind or had dealt with mouse issues before.

By this time, Tiger had run the mouse into the utility room. Elma cringed when she heard a thud. A few seconds later, the cat appeared, carrying the rodent in his mouth. The women giggled as the cat sat before them, apparently waiting for their approval. Even Elma thought it was rather cute.

"Good work, kitty." Sadie jerked the back door open. "Now take your prize outside."

As if he understood, Tiger bounded out the door.

"Don't worry," Sadie assured Elma. "We get mice at our place from time to time too. That's why we keep a few katze around."

Desperate for a change of subject, Elma said, "Maybe we should head back to the store and see what the others are doing."

When they entered the store, Elma saw Thelma on the floor reading to the children. They seemed to be totally engrossed as she read about a young boy named Solomon. Even the children's mothers, who stood nearby, listened. This was nothing new. Elma remembered how many times in their store back home, her sister had entertained some of the little ones while their mothers shopped. It was a nice gesture, but Elma hoped Thelma wouldn't get into the habit of doing that here. They had only the two of them running the store, so they both needed to wait on people.

That evening, after the supper dishes were done, the twins built a fire in the fireplace and settled into the living room to relax. Thelma picked up her knitting to work on Mom's gloves, when Elma suggested they try one of the desserts they'd been given today. She went to the kitchen and returned with a bunch of peanut butter cookies on a crystal platter Grandma had often used when the twins had come to visit. Thelma remembered it well because of a small chip on one corner.

"I have some water heating on the stove for tea." Elma placed the platter on the coffee table. "Is the gas lamp giving you enough light?"

"Jah, it's plenty."

"It looks like you're squinting. Would you like to borrow my reading glasses?"

Thelma shook her head. "No, I'm fine."

The teakettle whistled, and Elma returned to the kitchen.

"Do you need any help?" Thelma called.

"I can manage."

While her sister was getting the tea, Thelma put her knitting down and glanced around. With the exception of the linoleum in the kitchen and bathroom, the rooms in this house had hardwood floors.

Her gaze came to rest on the small table beside her chair, draped with one of Grandma's handmade doilies. This old house had a story to tell—their grandparents' story. Each piece of furniture and every room held a special memory. To Thelma it felt like a second home. She was anxious to see what new memories she and Elma would make here.

When Elma returned with two cups, she handed one to Thelma and took a seat on the sofa. "I'd like to discuss something with you."

Thelma tilted her head. "What's that?"

"Remember how at our folks' store, you often entertained the kinner who came in with their parents?"

"Like I did today. Those children were so cute. I think they really enjoyed the story."

"I'm sure they did, but there are only two of us running the store." Elma leaned slightly forward. "I think it would be best if we both stick to waiting on customers and let the parents deal with their children."

Thelma's shoulders slumped. "I'm sorry. I'll try to remember that." Her sister was right, but oh, how she would miss spending time with the children. Taking over Grandma and Grandpa's store meant more responsibilities for her and Elma. Things would be different from now on. Back home in their parents' store, Thelma had always mixed a bit of fun with work. She hoped, even though it was only the two of them now, that the fun wouldn't be completely lost.

"I appreciate that," Elma said. "So how would you like to go shopping tomorrow in Shipshe?"

Thelma smiled, remembering how often Grandpa had used that shortened version of the name Shipshewana. The town had several good places to shop and eat. "That's a good idea." She reached for a cookie. "Maybe I'll look for the paint we need."

Elma smiled. "I could use a new pair of shoes. Of course, they'll have to be on sale."

Thelma took a sip of tea. "There's one thing we need to consider."

"What's that?"

"Shipshe's ten miles away. It's a bit far to ride our bikes. That means we'll have to get out Grandma and Grandpa's old buggy and take—"

"Rusty," they said in unison.

Elma frowned. "We haven't used him yet. I hope that horse behaves himself."

Chapter 4

The next morning, Elma was surprised to see Tiger lying under the kitchen table. He looked a bit better since Thelma had brushed him the evening before. She'd thought her sister had put the cat out before they went to bed last night. But at least he'd slept in the kitchen, where they'd already seen two mice.

When Elma reached under the table, the cat opened his eyes and stretched. "Come on, Tiger, out you go. You're not going to stay in the house while Thelma and I are shopping today."

Elma picked up Tiger, opened the back door, and set him on the porch. She stopped for a moment to take a deep breath of cold air. Was that frost she saw on the grass? Could the warmer days of summer be gone already?

She grabbed an armful of wood and hauled it inside to feed the woodstove. Elma rubbed her arms. The overnight temperatures had dropped, leaving it a bit chilly inside. Soon, the pleasant sound of wood snapping and popping filled the air. A sudden wave of sadness flowed over her. She thought about all the times she and Thelma had warmed themselves in front of this stove when they were children. Grabbing the edge of her apron, she wiped her eyes. Elma didn't think she'd ever get used to cooking or baking in the old relic. Due to their lack of money right now, it could be some time before they'd be able to buy a stove like they had at home. But at least this one heated the kitchen. *Maybe that's why Grandpa and Grandma held on to this old thing. Grandma had gotten used to cooking on it, and it does possess a certain unique charm.*

After Elma was sure the fire was going, she got out the loaf of banana bread one of the women had given them yesterday. It would go well with the eggs she'd boiled last night, along with a cup of hot tea.

As Elma set the table, she rubbed her fingers over one of the plates. Another memory flashed across her mind. Grandma always made fluffy pancakes when the family came to visit. Pancakes were one of Elma's favorite breakfast foods. When she was younger, she often ate as many as six for breakfast. "I'll have to see if I can find Grandma's recipe," she murmured.

Her thoughts turned to how things had turned out after she and Thelma had found customers waiting at the store yesterday afternoon. It was nice to get acquainted with some of the women from their area, and even nicer to know that they lived in such a caring community. Elma was pleased to have met such kind ladies. How glad she was that they hadn't made an issue of Tiger chasing that mouse. *Maybe I shouldn't have worried about it either. I know I can be a bit fussy sometimes.*

When Elma first realized that some of the women wanted to shop, she wasn't too happy about it. She and Thelma still hadn't cleaned or organized much, not to mention taking inventory. But after reminding herself that they needed some money coming in, she'd gratefully accepted their cash and checks. Since the news was out that the twins had inherited their grandparents' store, she figured the best thing to do was keep the store open during the weekdays. They could reorder supplies and do their cleaning and organizing in the evenings. Of course Thelma, who was taking a shower right now, had other thoughts about that. She'd made it clear that she wanted her evenings free to knit or do other things. Thelma even said she didn't think the store was as bad as Elma thought. She couldn't see any need to organize, since their customers probably knew where things were already. Elma didn't agree.

Knowing she needed to get busy, Elma checked the firebox on the stove. It had heated up nicely, and the kitchen was getting warmer. Now if Thelma would get here, they could eat breakfast and get on with their day. They'd decided to put the CLOSED sign in the store window today, and she was anxious to leave for Shipshe. Then later, if there was time, she hoped to sort through some things in their store to see what may have expired and need to be thrown away.

A bloodcurdling scream reached the kitchen. Dropping the silverware on the table, Elma raced from the room and dashed down the hall. "Thelma, what's wrong?" she hollered, pounding on the bathroom door.

"Except for the cold water that was running down on me, I'm okay." Thelma's voice boomed through the closed door. "It went from lukewarm to ice cold. Let me tell you: it's the coldest and quickest shower I've ever had to take."

"Sorry. When you screamed, I was worried that you'd been hurt."

"No, I'm fine—just feel like I'm gonna freeze to death."

Elma sighed with relief. She was glad Thelma wasn't in serious danger, but they did need to address their inadequate hot water supply. "I have breakfast ready," Elma said through the door. "So unless you need something, I'll see you in the kitchen."

"Go ahead. I'll be there shortly."

When Thelma entered the kitchen a short time later, she was still shivering. "Did the water turn cold like that when you took your shower?" she asked.

Elma shook her head. "No, but it wasn't hot either. I wonder if the water tank may be going out."

"One more thing we'll have to fix." Thelma rubbed

her hands over her arms. "Look at me. My arms are full of goose bumps."

"Put this on." Elma grabbed a sweater and handed it to Thelma. "You may want to stand by the stove. It's warming up nicely in here."

"Is that frost I see out the window?" Thelma asked before slipping into the sweater and moving closer to the stove.

"Seems to be. I think we'll be seeing fewer warm, summery days now that fall is approaching."

"At least this old stove is good for something." Thelma scooted closer to the source of heat.

"Jah, but if we get more money coming in soon, I'd really like to replace it." Elma took a seat at the table. "I have everything set out, so whenever you're warm enough we can eat breakfast."

Thelma stood near the stove a few more minutes then joined Elma. Bowing her head, she silently prayed, *Heavenly Father, thank You for this food and the hands that prepared it. Please keep us safe as we travel to Shipshe today, and let this be a good day. Amen.*

LaGrange, Indiana

Joseph Beechy opened the door to his harness shop and drew in a deep breath. The odor of leather and pungent dye filled the room. These were aromas he was accustomed to, as he'd been making and repairing harnesses and other leather items since he'd graduated from the eighth grade. Of course, that had been a good many years ago, since Joseph would be turning thirty-eight the first week of December.

"Thirty-eight years old and still a bachelor," Joseph muttered as he turned on the gas lamps overhead. "Guess I'm destined to remain single."

It was hard to admit, but Joseph had never developed a serious relationship with any of the young women he'd known. He had been interested in a few of them; although his shyness had always gotten in the way. His face would heat up and he'd start to stutter whenever he approached any single women who'd caught his eye. Maybe it was best that he'd never married. Life was less complicated that way—although he did long for a wife and children and had even prayed for that.

Maybe it's my ears women don't like, he thought, tugging on one of his earlobes. Though Joseph's ears were an average size, they stuck out slightly. He'd always been self-conscious about them. Of course, it hadn't helped that some of the scholars who'd attended school with him made fun of his ears. They never dared to do it when the teacher was around, but that hadn't stopped them from teasing Joseph when they had Joseph alone. Had it not been for his older brother, Eli, standing up for him, Joseph would have probably been taunted even more.

Eli and their sister, Katie, were both married and each had four children. As much as Joseph enjoyed spending time with his nieces and nephews, he felt left out. It was a reminder that he'd probably never have a family of his own. Of course, if Joseph should ever find the woman of his dreams, he might step out of his comfort zone and at least try to approach her without making a fool of himself. *Finding the woman of my dreams? That'll probably never happen.*

Joseph's gaze came to rest on the loosely rolled leather pouring out of the shelves along one side of his shop. In an area near his workbench, bits of leather scraps lay piled on the cement floor. If his mother walked in right now, she would probably scold Joseph for not cleaning up after himself. Since this was his place of business, he figured he had the right to decide how it should look. Maybe that was another good thing about not being married. If he had a wife, she might come into the shop and tell him to clean the place up.

Moving over to some open boxes full of snaps, rings,

buckles, and rivets, Joseph rolled up his shirtsleeves, deciding that he needed to quit thinking and get to work. He'd connected the breast strap of a harness to a large three-way snap, when his good friend Delbert Gingerich entered the shop.

Delbert's long legs took him quickly across the room. "*Wie geht's?*" he asked, stepping over a pile of dirty leather straps and buckles.

"I'm doin' fairly well, Dell. How about yourself?"

"Can't complain." Delbert gestured to the harness Joseph held. "Looks like you're hard at work here, Joe."

"As a matter of fact, I'm just gettin' started." Joseph grinned. He and Delbert had been friends since they were teenagers. When Delbert started calling him "Joe," he'd given his friend the nickname "Dell." Since neither of them was married, they often did things together, like fishing, playing horseshoes, or having a good game of Ping-Pong. Of course Delbert, having longer, stronger arms, usually won at horseshoes. But Joseph almost always caught the biggest fish. While the men shared common interests, they had very different personalities and appearances. Delbert had blond hair, sky-blue eyes, and dimples that would turn any woman's head. Joseph's red hair and freckles made him feel homely in comparison, but that didn't matter much since Delbert seemed more interested in making his woodworking business successful than in looking for a wife. And while Delbert was outgoing and competitive, Joseph was timid and didn't care whether he won or lost at most games they played.

"What brings you by this morning?" Joseph asked.

Delbert snapped his suspenders. "I'm heading to Shipshe to pick up a few things and thought you might like to go along for the ride."

Joseph shook his head. "I've got too much to do here to be going on any joyrides."

"I'll treat you to lunch." He thumped Joseph's back. "How's that sound?"

"Where are you planning to eat?"

Delbert shrugged. "Oh, I don't know. I'm thinking maybe the Blue Gate."

Joseph looked down at the stain on his trousers. "Naw, that place is too nice for a working fellow like me."

"How about Wana Cup Restaurant? It's fairly casual."

"Jah, and they do have some pretty good pies and homemade ice cream."

Delbert bobbed his head. "That's right, they sure do. So are you willing to leave your work for a while and go to Shipshe with me?"

"Jah, sure, why not?" He set the harness on the workbench. "My work will be waiting for me when I get back."

As she and Thelma headed for Shipshewana in their grandparents' closed-in buggy, Elma gripped Rusty's reins. Grandpa's open buggy, which he and Grandma had been riding in when their accident occurred, had been demolished. Thinking about it now sent shivers up Elma's spine. She'd give anything if she could bring her grandparents back and make everything as it once was. *I still wonder why they left their home, the store, and all their possessions to me and Thelma. I wish that would have been stated in their will.*

"What are you thinking about?" Thelma asked, breaking into Elma's thoughts.

"How do you know I was thinking about anything?"

Thelma gave Elma a gentle nudge. "You had that 'I'm mulling things over' look."

Elma snickered. "Since you know me that well, maybe you can figure out what I was thinking."

"Grandma and Grandpa?"

"Jah. Riding in their buggy makes me miss them even more."

"I know what you mean." Thelma gestured to the horse. "At least Rusty's cooperating."

As if he had heard her, the horse picked up speed.

Elma tried to hold him back, but a car coming from the opposite direction honked, causing Rusty to go wild. When the horse darted into the other lane, she screamed. A vision of her grandparents flashed before her eyes. Was this what it was like before their buggy got hit? Elma knew if she didn't get control of the horse, they were going to collide with the oncoming car.

Chapter 5

Rusty's hooves slammed down on the pavement. He whinnied then shook his head with force as steam surged from his flaring nostrils. Elma's heart pounded as she gripped the reins with all her might, trying to guide him back to the right side of the road. The stubborn horse planted his feet firmly and wouldn't budge. She could almost hear her father's voice telling her to hold on tight and let Rusty know who was boss. Fortunately, the oncoming car had pulled over to the side of the road and stopped.

Elma had been around horses since she was a girl. She and Thelma had been given a pony and a cart for their tenth birthday. They'd begun driving a full-size horse and buggy by their early teens. But she'd never been this frightened or felt that she had so little control. Struggling with a sense of panic, Elma looked at her sister. "I can't make him go."

"Let me see what I can do." Thelma hopped out of the buggy and grabbed the horse's bridle. Rusty kept trying to shake his head, but Thelma held firm, while talking to him in a calm tone and stroking his side. Eventually, she was able to lead him and the buggy to the right-hand shoulder of the road.

The car moved on, and Elma breathed a sigh of relief. Her hands shook so hard she could barely hold on to the reins. She didn't want to go to Shipshewana now, but turning the horse around and heading back home was frightening too. What if Rusty acted up again? The next time it might not end so well.

Thelma opened the door on Elma's side of the buggy. "Slide over, Sister. I'll take over now. I can see that you need a break."

"Maybe we should go home and forget about shopping. I'm not sure we can trust Rusty to get us to Shipshe."

"We'll be fine. He needs to know who's in control. Besides, this is Rusty's first trip out since we moved here, and he's not used to us yet. We'll have to use him more and our bikes less."

Elma slid to the passenger's side and handed Thelma the reins. Closing her eyes, she prayed, asking God to give them a safe trip.

With an air of confidence, Thelma directed Rusty onto the road. So far, the horse was behaving himself, but Elma kept praying. Thelma had always been the braver one, but in the past, they'd both done well with horses. Now, Elma wasn't sure she could ever drive Rusty again. It was a good thing the woman who'd driven them from Sullivan to Topeka had a van, so they'd been able to bring their bikes. Despite what Thelma said, Elma planned on using her bicycle for her main mode of transportation. Of course, she wouldn't be able to ride it when the weather turned bad or if she had to travel a long ways.

She glanced over at Thelma and was amazed to see her relaxed expression. "I wonder if this cooler weather has anything to do with Rusty acting up. If it does, then with winter coming he'll probably get worse."

Thelma shook her head. "I don't think that's the horse's problem. He just needs a lot of work."

"None of our horses ever acted like that when we hooked them to our buggy. Maybe we ought to sell Rusty and have one of our horses from home brought to us."

"That would be expensive. I'm sure once we've worked with Rusty awhile, he'll be fine."

"I don't want to work with this horse." Elma shook

her head forcibly. "He's too spirited and unpredictable."

"Which will make him more of a challenge." Thelma's brows pulled in.

"Right. That's why we need to sell him."

Thelma let go of the reins with one hand and reached over to pat Elma's arm. "Let me take care of Rusty. I'm up to the challenge."

Shipshewana

When Thelma guided Rusty into the parking lot behind Yoder's Complex, she felt relief. She'd been able to get them the rest of the way without a problem, but she'd been nervous—although she hadn't let on to Elma. "Are you okay?" she asked her sister, noticing that her face was quite pale.

Elma slowly nodded. "I'm relieved to be here. You did an amazing job with Rusty. He didn't act up for you at all."

Thelma patted her sister's cold hand. "I did what needed to be done. Do you want to secure Rusty to the hitching rail, or shall I?"

"I'll take care of it." Elma stepped out of the buggy and walked up to Rusty.

As Thelma watched, she heard her sister scold the horse. "You scared me something awful. Don't ever do that again."

Rusty jerked his head back, pawed the pavement, and snorted.

Thelma knew Elma was afraid of the horse, but she had to get past it, or the animal would sense her fear and get worse.

Once Elma secured the horse, Thelma got out. "Where shall we go first?" she asked.

"I'd like to look in Yoder's Department Store for a pair of black dress shoes. When we were here two years ago, they had a good supply, so I'm hoping they'll have the plain style and size that I need. When I'm done there, I may run across the street to Spector's and see what kind of material they have."

"Why would you want to do that when we have material at our store?"

"We're getting low on some colors. If I find the color I want, I may buy enough to make a new dress. I still have some birthday money left."

"That's fine. While you're trying on shoes, I'll go across the hall to the hardware store and look for paint."

"Why don't we get something to drink first?" Elma suggested. "I could use a cup of herbal tea to help me relax."

The twins headed for Yoder's. After they'd ordered their tea, they sat in the restaurant and talked about all the things they'd need to do before their folks came to visit.

"It'll be great to see Mom and Dad again," Elma said. "But in some ways I wish they weren't coming so soon."

Thelma quirked an eyebrow. "Really? How come?"

"We haven't accomplished much of anything so far. Now that we're feeling the necessity of keeping the store open during the week, it's doubtful that we'll get much done at the house."

"We'll do what we can. I'm sure Mom and Dad won't expect everything to be perfect."

"I guess you're right, but I do want to show them that we've made some headway." Elma set her empty cup down at the same time as Thelma. "Are you ready to go shopping?"

Thelma chuckled. "Jah, sure. We can meet back at the buggy. After that, unless we want to do more shopping, we can go somewhere for lunch."

"Maybe we could stop over at Jo-Jo's and get a soft pretzel," Elma suggested. "That would be cheaper than buying a whole meal, and almost as filling."

"Okay. See you later."

When Thelma entered the hardware store, she spotted some puzzles. Thinking it could be fun for her and

Elma to work on one during cold winter evenings, she took one off the shelf. Placing it in her basket, she moved on to look at some bird feeders and seed. Grandma had always enjoyed watching the birds, and several feeders were hanging in the yard. Thelma had seen some birdseed in the barn yesterday, but she hadn't taken the time to fill any of the feeders. Maybe she'd do it when they got home later today.

Moving on, she noticed an Amish man with sandy-blond hair also looking at feeders. He was obviously not married because he had no beard. When he glanced her way, she quickly looked in another direction. She certainly didn't want him to catch her staring.

Remembering that they also needed some batteries, Thelma hurried off. When she located the right size for their flashlights, she added a package to her basket. She stopped to glance briefly at some sleds, but they wouldn't have need of anything like that until it snowed. When it did, if they found the time to go sledding, they could use the old ones hanging in Grandpa's barn.

Thelma had begun her search for paint, when she spotted two Amish women. One she didn't recognize, but the other woman was Sadie Yoder. "It's nice to see you again," Thelma said, walking over to Sadie.

Sadie smiled. "It's nice to see you too. Now, which twin are you?"

"I'm Thelma."

Sadie studied Thelma a few seconds, making her feel like a bug under a microscope. "I'm sure I'll remember who's who after I get to know you better. You and your sister look so much alike, it's hard to tell you apart."

"People have been getting us mixed up since we were kinner," Thelma responded.

"Is Elma here with you?" Sadie questioned.

"She's across the hall, looking for shoes."

"Oh, I see. Well Thelma, I'd like you to meet our bishop's wife, Lena Chupp. You didn't get to meet her the day of your grandparents' funeral because she was home with the flu."

The elderly woman smiled and greeted Thelma. "I'm sorry about your grandparents. They will be missed in our community." Thelma's throat constricted as Lena held on to her hand. "We're glad to have you and your sister in our church district and look forward to seeing you at the service this Sunday."

"Where will it be held?" Until now, Thelma hadn't thought about this Sunday and whether it would be a day of worship or an off-Sunday. Her only excuse was that she had so much on her mind.

"The service will be at Herschel Miller's," Sadie spoke up. "You met his wife, Doris, yesterday." She reached into her black leather purse and pulled out a tablet and pen. "I'll write their address down for you."

Thelma visited with the women a few more minutes, and after saying that she and Elma would see them on Sunday, she headed to the checkout counter to pay for her purchases.

As Thelma approached the counter, she was surprised to see the blond-haired Amish man waiting there as well. His arms were full, and she wondered why he hadn't picked up a basket to put his things in. An elderly man stood in front of him with several items. Since there was only one clerk, Thelma figured it could be several minutes before she or the blond man were waited on.

He kept fidgeting and glancing over his shoulder. Suddenly the man turned, bumping Thelma's arm.

"Oops. Sorry," he mumbled, trying to juggle the other items as the tape measure fell from his grasp. The next thing Thelma knew all of his purchases were on the floor.

Setting her basket down, Thelma leaned over to help him pick them up, but in doing so, they bumped heads.

"Sorry about that. Are you all right?" His shimmering blue eyes revealed the depth of his concern.

Rubbing her forehead, to be sure a lump wasn't

forming, Thelma could only manage a nod.

The man smiled, revealing deep dimples in both cheeks. "Guess this is my day for being clumsy. This morning, I dropped a carton of milk when I was fixing breakfast."

"It's okay. No harm done," Thelma murmured. It had been awhile since she'd met a man with such pretty blue eyes. They weren't an average shade of blue, like hers and Elma's. This man's eyes reminded her of a clear blue lake, glistening on a summer day.

He motioned to her basket. "Guess I should've gotten one of those instead of trying to carry everything myself."

Averting her gaze, Thelma reached for the tape measure still lying on the floor, but she ended up grasping his hand as he picked up the object.

"Oh, I'm sorry. It seems like I'm the clumsy one now." Thelma's face flooded with heat. "At least nothing appears to be broken."

"No, everything seems to be fine." He picked up the rest of his things and stood.

As Thelma clambered to her feet, she rubbed her hand down the side of her dress, still feeling the warmth from his hand when she'd accidently grasped it.

The older gentleman had finished checking out, so the blond-haired man put his purchases on the counter. After he paid for them, he gave Thelma a nod and left the store.

She paid for her things and was about to walk away, when she noticed a piece of paper on the floor. Thinking the man must have dropped it, she picked it up, but by then he was out of sight. *This looks interesting,* Thelma thought, realizing it was a flyer advertising a cooking show. The event would take place in Shipshewana the following month. Everything the contestants made would be auctioned off and go to the winning bidders. The proceeds would go to several families in the community with medical expenses. Since the Amish didn't carry health insurance, they relied on events such as this to help in emergencies. Thelma thought this might be something she and Elma should take part in. It was for a good cause, and since they were now part of the Amish community in this area, they should do something to help.

Delbert had crossed the street to meet Joseph for lunch, when he saw an Amish woman going into Spector's. He was surprised to see that it was the same young woman he'd bumped into at the hardware store. "That's strange. I thought she was wearing a green dress."

"Who were you talking to?" Joseph bumped Delbert's arm.

Startled, Delbert whirled around. "What are you doing sneaking up on me like that?"

"I wasn't sneaking. I finished what little shopping I decided to do and thought we were supposed to meet here before we went to lunch."

Delbert's face heated. "We were. . . . I mean. . ." He didn't know why he felt so flustered all of a sudden.

"So who were you talking to?" Joseph asked.

"No one. I mean, I was talking to myself." Delbert pointed to Spector's. "Did you see a woman go in there a few minutes ago?"

Joseph shook his head. "Nope. Can't say as I did."

"I bumped into her at Yoder's Hardware, and I thought she was wearing a green dress. But when I saw her again, I realized her dress was blue."

Joseph thumped Delbert's shoulder. "What's going on here, friend? Are you interested in that woman?"

"Course not. I don't even know her. Never saw her till today, in fact." Delbert scratched his head. "I wonder if she's married."

Joseph punched Delbert's arm. "Don't get any ideas. Remember, we're both confirmed bachelors."

Chapter 6

Topeka

"What are you thinking about, Thelma?" Elma asked as they ate breakfast Sunday morning. "You look like you're five hundred miles away."

Staring out the window, Thelma sighed and glanced back at her sister. "No, not five hundred—maybe ten miles or so."

Elma's eyebrows lifted. "What do you mean?"

"Oh, nothing." She picked up her glass of apple juice and took a drink. She wasn't about to tell Elma she'd seen an attractive Amish man at the hardware store the other day and couldn't quit thinking about him. Elma would tease her. Besides, it wasn't likely she'd see the man again, much less get to know him.

"You must have been thinking about something or you wouldn't have been staring off into space." Elma reached for the salt shaker and sprinkled some on her scrambled eggs. "But if you'd rather not talk about it, that's okay with me."

"It's nothing, really." Thelma didn't like where this conversation was headed, so she quickly changed the subject. "When we were in Shipshe the other day, I picked up some candy. Think I'll put it in my purse and hand it out to the kinner who are in church today."

Elma smiled. "The children in our church district in Sullivan always enjoyed it when you gave out candy, so I'm sure the ones here will like it too. By the way, did you get the paint you went after?"

"Uh-oh. Guess I got sidetracked and forgot. I'll have to make another trip to Shipshe sometime this week." Thelma went to get her purse from a wall peg near the back door. Then she grabbed the bag of candy from the cupboard. When she opened her purse to put the candy in, she noticed the cooking show flyer she'd put in there and forgotten about. "Look at this, Sister," she said, bringing it back to the table with her. "I found it on the floor in Yoder's Hardware the other day."

Elma took the flyer and put her reading glasses on. "'Shipshewana Cooking Show. All contestants who enter will have their baked or cooked item auctioned off.'" She removed her glasses and squinted as she looked at Thelma. "This looks interesting, but why are you showing it to me?"

"Didn't you read the rest of the flyer? The proceeds from the auction will help people in the community who have medical expenses. It's for a good cause."

Elma moved her head slowly up and down as she placed the piece of paper on the table. "I saw that, and if we have time we might go to the event and give a donation of whatever we can afford."

"Oh no," Thelma said, her excitement mounting as she thought more about this. "I think we should make something that will be auctioned off. We could make a dessert from Grandma's favorite recipe book."

"That's a nice thought, but with all we have to do here and at the store, we don't have the time for something like that."

Thelma motioned to the flyer. "The cooking show doesn't take place until the first Saturday of October, so we'd have almost a month to figure out what we want to make and get it done. We could take an evening, and instead of working on the puzzle, or me knitting, we could bake something. It wouldn't hurt for us to close the store that day either, so we could attend the event." Thelma paused to catch her breath then kept going with enthusiasm, her voice growing louder. "It would be a nice way for us to contribute to a good cause. I'm sure others in our community here in Topeka will be attending the show that day."

"You sound pretty excited about this. I'll give it some thought. Right now though, we need to finish our breakfast so we can be on our way to church." Elma drank the rest of her juice. "It wouldn't be good for us to be late on our first Sunday attending services here."

Thelma glanced at the battery-operated clock on the wall behind them, noting that it was only seven o'clock. "I'm sure we'll get there in plenty of time. By the way, did you find the shoes you were hunting for at the store in Shipshe?"

Elma stuck out her foot. "Jah. I'm wearing them. I also found some material for a new dress in the color I wanted."

"That's good to hear. At least one of us got what we went after."

Elma looked at the table and frowned. "I wish the Millers' place was close enough for us to walk." She picked up her readers and put them in her eyeglass case. "I can't say that I'm looking forward to going anywhere again with that unpredictable horse."

Thelma reached over and patted her sister's hand. "Not to worry. I'll be in the driver's seat the whole way." She leaned back in her chair, enjoying the warmth of the stove. The sun's light poured into the kitchen, adding a warm, golden glow. "I'll take charge of driving Rusty until you feel ready to sit in the driver's seat again."

Elma sighed. "That's a relief. After what happened with Rusty the other day, I'm in no hurry to drive again."

Thelma tipped her head. "Did you hear that noise?"

"What? I didn't hear anything."

"It sounded like a cat shrieking, and I think it was coming from the basement." Thelma stood. "Maybe we should go check."

"Why don't you go while I do the dishes? It's almost

time to leave for church, and if we both go to the basement, we'll have to leave the dishes till we get home this afternoon." Elma glanced at her new shoes. "Sure hope I chose the right size shoes. These are pinching my toes a bit."

"Sorry about that. Maybe you ought to take them back."

"No, I think they'll be okay once I break them in."

"Okay, whatever you think best. I'm gonna run down to the basement and check on that noise."

Thelma grabbed a flashlight, clicked it on, and started down the basement steps. When she reached the bottom, she turned on one of the gas lamps. Nothing seemed out of the ordinary. It was quiet. *That's sure strange. I was almost sure I heard a cat.*

"Tiger, are you down here?" She clapped her hands. "Here, kitty, kitty."

No response.

Holding the flashlight in front of her and swatting a few cobwebs out of the way, Thelma began searching, while calling for the cat. *I guess one of these days we'll have to clean this basement, or the spiders are going to take over.*

Behind the stairs, she still saw nothing then ducked, but it was too late. "Eww. . ." She'd walked headlong into a dirty web. Quickly, she pulled away the silken strands gummed to her cap and forehead. "Come on, kitty. Where are you?" she called again. "You don't have to hide from me." If it was Tiger, the friendliest of all the cats, she was sure he would have responded—unless he was trapped.

"Here, kitty. Where are you, kitty?" Thelma stood still and listened, but except for her sister humming upstairs and the sound of water flowing through the pipes, she still heard nothing. Her nose twitched. *This place smells like a combination of dust and mildew. It really needs a thorough cleaning.*

"Thelma, are you coming?" Elma shouted from above. "If we don't leave now, we are definitely going to be late!"

"Okay, I'm on my way." Thelma headed up the stairs, wondering if she had imagined the noise.

Back in the kitchen, she'd put the flashlight away and had turned to head out of the room, when Elma pointed at her. "You must have brushed against something downstairs. There's a smudge on your dress."

Thelma brushed it away. "Looks like dust. There are plenty of cobwebs in the basement. Someday we'll need to go down there and clean."

"We'll add that to our ever-growing list of to-dos." Elma sighed. "Before we go, did you remember to turn off the gas lamp in the basement?"

Thelma bobbed her head. "At least, I think I did." She tapped her chin. "You know, I can't remember doing that. I'd better run back down and make sure it's off."

Elma sighed. "Really, Sister, I wish you would try to stay a little more focused."

"Sorry about that. I was listening for the noise I heard. Plus trying not to eat any spiders," she added under her breath.

"Did you find out what it was?"

"No, I didn't hear it again, and when I looked around with the flashlight, I didn't see anything out of the ordinary either." Before Elma could comment, Thelma grabbed the flashlight and headed back downstairs.

As soon as Thelma reached the bottom, she saw that she had left the gas lamp on. She reached up to turn it off, when she heard that same catlike screech. The sound came from way back in one corner of the basement. Shining her flashlight, she discovered one of the cats in a small wooden box full of rags. Beside it was a tiny kitten, and it appeared as if the little one had recently been born. No doubt, the mama cat would deliver more babies soon.

Thelma clasped her hand over her mouth. *Oh my! If Elma finds out about this, she'll want to move the cats out to the barn. Well, she can't know. I'll have to keep it a secret and find a way to keep Elma from coming down here until the cats are old enough to go outside. Maybe I shouldn't have said anything about cleaning the basement.*

As the twins headed for church with their unpredictable horse, Elma tried to relax. Rusty was doing much better for Thelma than he had done for her the other day. *He must have sensed my fear,* Elma thought. *I'm glad my sister isn't afraid and was willing to drive.* The thought of sitting in the driver's seat, trying to keep control of the horse they'd inherited sent shivers up the back of Elma's neck. She knew she had to get past her fear or she'd never be able to drive their buggy, but right now she couldn't deal with that. Maybe once Thelma got Rusty tamed a bit, Elma would try taking him out again. Of course, she'd make sure her sister was along, in case there was a problem.

As they approached the Millers' home, Rusty picked up speed. He'd apparently gone there before with Grandpa in the driver's seat and was anxious to get there again. It made Elma wonder if Rusty was anxious to see some special horse at the Millers'.

Even with her nervousness over the horse, she noticed how pretty the Millers' farm was, nestled back in, off the road.

"Can't you make him go any slower?" Elma asked as Thelma directed the horse up the driveway. "Look at the dust he's kicking up behind us. People will think we're crazy, approaching like this."

"I'm trying to, but Rusty seems quite excited."

Elma noticed that her sister was holding the reins pretty tight, and it looked like she was gritting her teeth. Maybe she wasn't as confident driving this aggravating horse as she'd let on.

"Whoa, Rusty!" The twins called in unison.

Thelma pulled back on the reins, and the horse came to a stop a foot or so from the barn. She looked over at Elma and smiled. "We're here!"

Elma released a quick breath. "Jah, and thank the Lord we didn't run into the barn."

After one of the young men came up to greet them and took Rusty away to be watered and stabled, Elma walked across the yard with Thelma. Several women were clustered outside on the lawn near a large white building that Elma assumed was Mr. Miller's workshop. A group of men stood chatting in a line on the other side of the shop door.

As the twins were greeted by each of the women, Elma recognized several from the day of their grandparents' funeral. Sadie Yoder introduced Elma to Lena Chupp and Lena introduced the twins to the other women they didn't know.

Shortly before nine o'clock, they entered the shop and took their seats. At a quick glance, Elma could see the shop was as neat and orderly inside as it was outside. It had obviously been thoroughly cleaned before the benches were set up for service.

Soon after, the men came in. The ministers and older men entered first, followed by young married men, and then the youth and young boys. The men sat on the opposite side of the room from the women, facing one another.

The service began with a song from their ancient Amish hymnal, the *Ausbund*. One of the men led off, carrying the first few notes, and then everyone else joined him. Soon after the singing began, the ministers left the building to discuss who would preach and to offer instructional classes to any candidates for baptism. An hour or so later, the ministers returned. When the singing ended a short time later, the first minister rose to begin his sermon, which lasted about twenty minutes. It still amazed Elma how the bishop and other ministers could preach without any notes on readings mostly found in the New Testament.

By the time the second minister, their bishop, rose to speak, Elma was struggling to keep from yawning out loud. She clasped her hand over her mouth and hoped no one was looking at her. They shouldn't be, after all;

everyone was supposed to be focused on the one delivering the message. With eyes feeling heavy, Elma's head lowered then bobbed up again. *Oh no, I can't fall asleep. Guess I shouldn't have stayed up so late last night working on that new puzzle Thelma bought. On top of that, I'm exhausted from everything we did this past week. It's all catching up with me, I guess.*

Elma glanced at Thelma. She seemed to be wide awake and listening intently to what Homer Chupp, the elderly bishop, was saying. He was preaching from the book of Luke, chapter 18, and had quoted verse 27, which Elma had read the other day: "And he said, The things which are impossible with men are possible with God."

Given everything she and her sister were facing, Elma needed the reminder that nothing was impossible with God. They would try to do their best, seek His wisdom in all their business dealings, and trust Him to take care of their needs.

As the bishop's message continued, Elma struggled to keep her eyes open. At one point she was about to nod off, when Thelma's elbow connected with her arm. Elma's eyes snapped open and she sat up straight. She hoped she hadn't missed anything important. *What am I thinking?* she asked herself. *Everything that happens during our three-hour Sunday services is important—especially the Bible verses that are quoted during the message.*

Elma did better after that, but by the time Homer Chupp's message was over and the last song had been sung, she felt drowsy again. Hopefully after the meal, she and Thelma could be on their way home, because Elma needed a nap.

When it came time for the twins to sit down to the light meal that had been prepared, Elma felt a headache coming on. She didn't say anything, however, because Thelma seemed so eager to visit and make new friends. As soon as Thelma finished eating a few pieces of bread, spread with sweetened peanut butter, she offered to hold a young woman's baby so the mother could eat with both hands free. After putting some peanut butter on her own piece of bread, Elma realized that she wasn't the least bit hungry. Out of politeness, she nibbled on the bread, but set it down and took a sip of water instead. As the pain increased, she brought her hand up to the back of her neck and massaged it for a bit. It didn't help much, and she felt more uncomfortable by the minute.

When the woman who'd introduced herself as Nancy finished eating and took the baby back, Elma leaned over and whispered to Thelma, "Are you ready to leave now? I'd like to go home and take a nap."

"In a minute," Thelma said. "I haven't given out the candy I brought to any of the kinner." She hopped up and headed across the yard to where a group of children played a game of tag. They stopped immediately when she showed them the bag of candy, and it wasn't long before several more children showed up. Once all the candy had been passed out, Thelma went over to the swing set and started pushing one of the little girls who'd been at the store this past week.

Elma groaned inwardly, while rubbing her forehead. At this rate, they'd never get home. She feared that if they didn't leave soon, she could lose what little was in her stomach, because what had started out to be a normal headache was now turning into a pounding migraine.

Nancy leaned over and asked, "Are you all right? You look pale, and I noticed you rubbing your head."

"I've been fighting a *koppweh*, and it's turned into a migraine," Elma admitted.

Doris Miller came over. "Why don't you go inside and lie down for a while? You can rest in the downstairs guest room."

"I appreciate the offer, but I think it would be best if my sister and I head for home."

Elma told the women good-bye and headed across the yard to where Thelma was visiting with the children.

"Sorry for interrupting, but I'm not feeling well. We need to go home."

"Oh, I'm sorry, Elma; I didn't know. I'll see about getting the horse right away."

Thelma hurried off and Elma headed straight for the buggy. When she got inside, she took her sunglasses out of her purse. The glare of the sun was intense and magnified the throbbing in her head. She blinked her eyes rapidly. Even her vision was blurring. Holding her stomach as a wave of nausea coursed through it, she hoped Thelma would return soon.

Elma moaned. *Why now?* She had hoped to enjoy today, since it was their first church service here and a chance to meet more of those in their community. Now, as she waited in the buggy, trying to think of things besides the pain in her head, waves of haziness clouded her vision. She closed her eyes to ward off the dizziness. *What is taking my sister so long? I hope she hasn't stopped to talk to anyone.*

Several minutes later, Thelma led Rusty to the front of the buggy. The same Amish boy who had greeted them this morning was with her. He took care of getting the horse hitched while Thelma climbed into the driver's seat.

As they headed down the driveway, Elma's stomach gave a lurch. "Sister, you'd better pull over. I'm gonna be sick."

Chapter 7

Kotz es raus, no fiehlscht besser!" Thelma hollered as her sister bent over a clump of weeds. She'd told Elma to vomit it out, knowing it would make her feel better. Of course, it might not do much for her headache.

When Elma returned to the buggy a few minutes later, her face was pale as goat's milk. "I'm glad I didn't do that in front of the others. It would have been so humiliating."

"I'm sorry you're not feeling well. When we get home, you should go straight to bed."

"I surely won't argue with that. Resting in a darkened room is the only way I'll be able to get rid of this headache."

Thelma gave Elma's arm a gentle pat. "Don't worry about anything. As soon as we get home, you can head to the house. I'll take care of Rusty's needs and feed the chickens, as well as the cats. We were in such a hurry this morning, I forgot to do that."

"Danki." Elma leaned her head back and closed her eyes. Thelma hoped they'd make it home without her sister getting sick to her stomach again.

Please, Lord, let Rusty behave himself on the way home, Thelma silently prayed as she directed the horse onto the main road. With Elma feeling so poorly, this would not be a good time for him to act up.

When Thelma guided Rusty into their yard, Elma felt relieved. Not only had the horse obeyed Thelma's commands, but Elma was simply glad to be home. Her stomach still churned a bit, and her head felt like it could explode, but at least she could finally lie down in her room. As soon as Thelma pulled Rusty to the hitching rail, Elma climbed out of the buggy. As hard as this simple task was, she managed to quickly secure the horse then gave her sister a wave and headed for the house. She walked slowly, not only because each step she took seemed to intensify the pain but also because she felt wobbly from the dizziness.

Stepping onto the porch, she was greeted by Tiger meowing and rubbing against her leg. "Go away," she muttered. "I'm not going to pet you, and you're not coming in."

Elma opened the door and slipped inside before the cat could make its move. She wished they'd never started letting him in at all, because now he expected it. *If we see any more mice, then he can come in,* Elma thought as she hung her black outer bonnet on a wall peg.

She went to the kitchen and got a glass of water then made her way carefully up the stairs. When she entered her room, she took off her dress and slipped into her nightgown. After she'd released her hair from its bun, she crawled into bed. Sleep was what she needed—quiet, uninterrupted sleep.

Elma was on the verge of dozing off, when Thelma tapped on her door. "Are you okay? Do you need anything? Should I fix you a cup of tea?"

Elma groaned. "No thanks. I just need some sleep."

"Oh, all right. I'm going downstairs now, but I'll check on you later."

Elma knew her sister meant well, but she wished she hadn't bothered her. Thelma wasn't prone to migraines, so she didn't fully understand what they were like. For Elma, they usually came on when she hadn't had enough sleep or was really stressed about something. She certainly had plenty of reasons to feel anxious right now—not only about the store and the home they'd inherited but also about their unpredictable horse.

As Thelma moved through the hall, past both her and Elma's bedrooms, her gaze came to rest on the large jar of marbles sitting on the floor at the end of the hall. Grandpa had collected marbles and had several jars scattered around the house. Some were in the way, as this one was.

Think I'll move that jar into the spare bedroom for now, Thelma decided. *Elma and I can decide what to do with it later on, but at least it won't be a danger to us anymore.*

At first, Thelma tried to lift the cumbersome jar, but it was too heavy. *Maybe I'll try to slide it over there.* Leaning over, she grabbed the top of the jar and tipped it slightly in order to get a good grip. Moving backward, she slid it across the floor. She was almost to the guest room when she realized the door was closed. Trying to steady the jar with one hand, she reached up with the other hand to open the door. She turned the knob, but it wouldn't open. Then she remembered that this particular door had a tendency to stick. She pushed again, a little harder. As the door suddenly gave way, Thelma lost her balance, and the jar slipped from her grasp, crashing to the floor. Fortunately, the jar was intact, but marbles of all sizes and colors rolled everywhere along the hardwood floor, some even bouncing down the stairs.

Thelma's finger went to her lips, as if that would somehow muffle the racket and not disturb her sister. Thelma watched helplessly as the marbles finally rolled to a stop. Hunching her shoulders and holding her breath as everything grew quiet again, she squeezed her eyes shut and waited.

"What's going on out there?" Elma called from her room.

"Don't come out!" Thelma hollered, wishing her sister hadn't been disturbed. "I dropped a jar, and marbles are everywhere. It's not safe. Let me sweep the marbles into the guest room and pick up the strays. I'll let you know when it's safe to come out."

"Okay. Be careful, Thelma. You don't want to slip and fall."

"I'll watch what I'm doing."

"Do you need any help?"

"No, I can manage. Please, stay in your room and rest." Thankful that they had a broom in the upstairs utility closet, Thelma took it out. After she'd opened the door to the spare room, she laid a small cardboard box on its side and swept the marbles inside. She would figure out what to do with them some other time.

Looking around the room at the boxes and other items scattered about, Thelma realized they would never have it cleaned up in time for Mom and Dad to sleep here. They'd have to use Grandma and Grandpa's old room downstairs. That would be more convenient anyway, since it was close to the bathroom. She hoped it wouldn't make Dad feel sad to sleep in his parents' bed.

After Thelma had picked up the stray marbles that had rolled down the steps, she headed outside to the coop to feed the chickens and check for eggs. When that was done, she set the basket filled with six eggs on the back porch and headed across the yard.

Breathing the earthy scent lingering in the air, Thelma headed toward the barn. Even though it was in need of a new coat of red paint, the building itself would probably be around for a good many years.

When she entered the barn and headed for Rusty's stall, he kicked the wall in front of him. "Now calm down, boy. Your meal is on the way." Thelma grabbed a hefty chunk of alfalfa hay and placed it in the horse's feeding trough. "How's it going, Rusty?"

The horse nickered.

Thelma smiled and patted him gently up by his ear. "It's your dinnertime, and now the barn cats need some food too." She left his stall, making sure the latch was secure on his door.

After she'd fed and watered the cats, she took a seat on a bale of straw. Leaning against another bale, she sat quietly listening and watching the animals crunching on their food. They all appeared to be content, like she was, breathing in the pleasant grassy aroma in the barn. Thelma missed the way things had been when her grandparents were living. Looking over at Cutter's empty stall made this moment quite difficult to bear. She fought back tears as she continued to sit and reminisce. Finally, she rose, brushed her sweater and dress off, and headed back to the house.

Once inside, she took care of the eggs then fixed herself a glass of chocolate milk and went to the living room to relax. The past week had been busy, and it was nice sitting here in the quiet and solitude.

Thelma reached for Grandma's Bible lying on the table beside her. Opening it to a page marked with a ribbon, she read Proverbs 16:20 out loud: " 'He that handleth a matter wisely shall find good: and whoso trusteth in the LORD, happy is he.' "

What a good verse this is for us right now, Thelma thought. *I need to commit it to memory.*

Hearing a noise from below, Thelma suddenly remembered the mother cat and baby she'd found in the basement. She needed to check on them and feed the mama cat.

Setting the Bible aside and slipping into her sweater again, Thelma went back out to the barn. When she returned to the house, she was relieved to see that Elma hadn't gotten up yet. It wouldn't be good if she had to explain what she was doing with a sack of cat food. She'd never understood why her sister didn't care much for cats.

Thelma went to the kitchen and grabbed her flashlight then made her way down to the basement. As soon as she descended the last step, she heard mewing. Taking a quick peek, she saw that the mama cat now had four babies. "I brought you some nourishment, Misty." Thelma chose that name because the cat had light gray fur. She poured food into the dish she'd brought along and set it near Misty. The cat sniffed it and then started chomping. While Misty ate, Thelma filled another bowl with water from the utility sink. Some dirty clothes were in the laundry basket, and Thelma was glad the cat hadn't climbed in that to give birth to her babies.

Passing the hot water tank on her way to give Misty her drink, Thelma noticed a small puddle. She hoped the tank wasn't leaking. Perhaps some water had sloshed out of the washing machine when she'd washed a few towels yesterday. But if that were the case, wouldn't there be moisture in other places too?

Thelma gave Misty a drink then grabbed an old rag and sopped up the water. If it had come from the old tank, it would probably happen again. She'd check it the next time she came down. Thelma sighed. *One more thing to remember.*

LaGrange

Joseph leaned back in his chair, locking his fingers behind his head as he visited with Delbert after the noon meal following the church service in their district. They'd stayed longer than usual today, enjoying the fellowship with members of their community.

"Those were good messages our ministers preached today," Joseph said. "The one our bishop preached about being trustworthy and keeping our promises really spoke to me."

Delbert nodded, stroking his chin. "The promises we render to unbelievers can make a difference in how they view us as Christians."

"That's true. If we say we're gonna do something and don't follow through, it makes us appear dishonest." Joseph reached for his coffee cup and took a drink. "The other sermon, about helping others when we see a need, was important too."

"Jah."

"Speaking of helping others," Joseph said, "when we were in Shipshe the other day, I picked up a flyer about a cooking show that will take place next month. It's for a good cause. Would you like to go there with me?"

Delbert grinned. "You know, now that you mentioned it, I picked up the same flyer. I must have dropped it somewhere though, 'cause when I got home, it wasn't with my purchases."

"Did you plan to go?"

"Sure, if something else doesn't come up."

Joseph snapped his fingers. "Say, I have an idea. Since you're a pretty fair cook, maybe you could make something and have it auctioned off."

"No way! I'd have to not only make something ahead of time and bring it to the event, but I'd be required to stand in front of everyone and make the recipe from scratch." Delbert shook his head vigorously. "I wouldn't mind bringin' something to auction off, but I could never prepare it in front of a large crowd."

Joseph tapped his friend's arm. "Okay, Dell, forget I mentioned that part, but if you're not busy that day, you can join me, because I plan to go."

"Jah, okay." Delbert smiled. "As you said, it is for a good cause. Maybe we'll find something we'd both like to bid on that day."

Chapter 8

Topeka

The next morning, Thelma had breakfast ready when Elma entered the kitchen. "Did you sleep well?" Thelma asked. "Is your koppweh gone?"

Elma walked over to the window and looked out. "Jah, my headache is gone. It upsets me when I get a migraine like that, because it puts me down, sometimes for hours."

"I'm sorry you have to deal with those. I can't imagine what it must be like. Even when I get a sinus headache, it's rough."

Elma sat down at the table. "I'm glad headaches like that are one thing we don't have in common. I sure wouldn't want you to go through such pain—not to mention getting sick to your stomach."

"Thank the good Lord your headache is over. Shall we pray?"

Elma nodded, and they both bowed their heads. *Heavenly Father,* Thelma prayed, *please guide and direct our lives this week and keep our friends and family safe. Bless this food to the nourishment of our bodies. Amen.*

When they had both finished praying, Thelma smiled and handed her sister a bowl of oatmeal. "I hope this isn't too sticky. I think I'm getting the hang of cooking on top of the stove, but sometimes the kettle heats up too quickly and everything sticks to the bottom."

Elma added a pat of butter and some brown sugar to her bowl and stirred it around. Then she poured a little milk over the top and took a bite. "It tastes fine to me."

"Oh good." Thelma put butter in her bowl of cereal as well, only she added a hefty dash of cinnamon along with several scoops of brown sugar before finishing it off with milk.

Elma's brows wrinkled. "That's a lot of sugar you've added to your hot cereal."

"You're right; I probably shouldn't have gotten so carried away." Thelma grinned as she stirred the toppings into the oatmeal. "I wish we had some raisins to add. That would be healthy and tasty."

"We'll get some the next time we go for groceries," Elma said. "As soon as we're finished eating though, I think I'll go down to the basement and wash some clothes before it's time to open the store. Since it's raining lightly this morning, I'll hang everything on the line in the basement."

Feeling a sense of panic, Thelma's grin faded, and her eyes widened. "There's no reason for you to do that. You had a rough day yesterday and need to take it easy. Let me do the laundry."

"After lying around most of yesterday, I'm anxious to do something." Elma cleared her throat. "Besides, I'm fine now, and since we'll be working in the store most of the day, I definitely won't be taking it easy."

"That may be true, but it's all the more reason to let me wash our clothes," Thelma insisted. If Elma went to the basement, she'd probably hear Misty or her kittens, and that was the last thing Thelma needed.

"Okay, if you insist." Elma drank some of her coffee. "While you're doing that, I'll go over some of my lists to make sure I haven't forgotten to write down anything important that needs to be done. Have you been adding things to your list?"

"I've been trying," Thelma replied. *Should I say anything about the puddle I found near the hot water tank? No, my sister will want to go down there and check on it herself. That would be another opportunity for her to discover the mama cat and her kittens. I'll wait.*

Thelma smiled. "When we're both done with our chores in here, we can head over to the store."

"What about the outside chores?" Elma questioned. "Do you want me to feed the chickens and gather eggs while you take care of the barn cats and Rusty?"

Thelma touched her sister's arm. "Already taken care of. I did those things while you were taking your shower."

"Jah, and a cold shower it was." Elma grimaced. "I had only been showering a few minutes before the water went from lukewarm to cold. I'm afraid it won't be long and we'll have to replace that old water tank in the basement."

"Maybe it only needs some adjustments or a new element," Thelma was quick to say. "We'll ask Dad to take a look at it after the folks get here next week."

Elma's eyes brightened. "I can't believe they'll be here so soon. Won't it be great to see them again?"

Thelma nodded. "I hope Mom doesn't try to talk us out of staying here. She wasn't too happy when she found out Grandpa and Grandma had left us their place."

"That's true, but she's had some time to get used to the idea, so maybe she won't even bring up the notion of us selling this place and moving back home." Elma blotted her lips with her napkin. "I hope not, because even though we've had a few bumps in the road, I already feel like this is our home."

"Me too. It's good that we're both in agreement because we could never do all this work without each other's help." Thelma spooned a small bite of cereal into her mouth. "Yum. This tastes *appeditlich*. Too bad it takes so much effort to cook on that old stove."

"You're right. It is delicious." Elma poured a little more milk over her oatmeal. "As the old saying goes, 'Anything good takes effort.'"

When Thelma got to the basement, she turned on the gas lamps then checked on the cats and gave the mama some food. She also made sure to give Misty a litter box filled with shredded newspapers she'd found stacked along one wall in the basement. It seemed that her grandparents liked to save everything.

Thelma stood watching the cute little kittens for a few minutes. Their eyes wouldn't open for at least ten days, but somehow they managed to wiggle their little bodies around. Moving over to the wringer washing machine, she started filling the tub with water and poured in the detergent. While the water went in, she put some sheets in the machine. The tub still had a lot of room, so she retrieved some dirty towels from the laundry basket and added them as well. Thelma leaned over and looked under the washer, making sure the hose was inside the floor drain. *Sure wouldn't want water running out the hose and having a big mess to mop up,* she thought.

"Do you need any help with the clothes?" Elma hollered down the basement stairs.

Thelma cupped her hands around her mouth. "Danki anyway, but I'm fine on my own. Keep doing what you're doing. I'll be up as soon as I get the clothes hung on the line."

Thelma watched the clothes agitating for a moment. Then she grabbed the broom and brushed away the cobwebs overhead as she moved around the washroom. Smiling, she was pleased that at least this area was a bit tidier.

Elma had put her notepad away when Thelma came upstairs. "It's still raining lightly, so we may need our umbrellas."

"Okay. I'll get one for each of us." Thelma went to the utility room and returned with two black umbrellas. She handed one to Elma and opened the back door.

"Looks like it might let up soon," Elma commented as they headed to the store. "See that blue patch of sky?" She pointed to the east.

"I see that, but even if it quits raining, it feels like it's going to be a chilly day. Oh, and look who's following us—Tiger the cat." Thelma's umbrella bumped into Elma's, knocking it out of her hand and onto the ground. "Oops! Sorry about that. Here, take mine." Thelma handed her umbrella to Elma, and then stepping around her, she grabbed the one that had fallen.

Elma smiled. "Danki. No harm done."

They stepped onto the porch, and when Elma unlocked the door, she paused. "We'll be inside most of the day, so we won't even notice the weather." She entered the store, and Thelma followed.

"It's a bit dampish in here." Thelma rubbed her arms. "I've got goose bumps already."

"Guess one of us should have come out earlier and gotten that little woodstove going."

"You know what?" Thelma whirled around. "One of us really needs to go out to the phone shack and check for messages."

"I suppose that would be a good idea," Elma agreed. "I'll go, unless you want to."

"No, you go ahead. I want to get this stove going so we have some heat in here. Then I need to do more inventory before any customers show up."

"Okay, I'll be back soon."

"Oh great!" Elma pointed. "You left the door open, and the cat got in. We'd better get him quick before he hides, or we'll be stuck with that critter in our store all day."

"I'll take care of it." Thelma scooped up the cat and carried him outside, along with her umbrella. "All's good," she said before closing the door behind her.

Elma put her umbrella behind the counter and saw a box of starter sticks to get a fire going. She'd also noticed a small pile of wood stacked outside by the side of the store. That must have been where Grandpa kept the wood they used for the stove.

Elma finished lighting a few of the fire sticks she'd put inside the stove and sniffed. Glancing back at the stove, she noticed smoke coming out through the door, and also from the area where the pipe connected. Quickly, she ran to the bathroom and filled a jar with water. Dashing back to the stove, she doused the fire. Luckily, it hadn't been burning long enough to make the stove or the pipe hot.

Elma wasn't sure she was doing the right thing, but she detached the pipe where it connected to the stove then twisted it off at the top where it connected to another section that went through the store's roof. "Let's see if there's anything blocking this straight part," she muttered, holding the pipe up and looking through it. Elma shrieked as an empty bird's nest fell onto the floor. Instinctively, she looked up the pipe, which was a big mistake. At that instant, a puff of soot swooshed onto her face.

"Ach no!" Elma sputtered, blowing a cloud of soot off her lips. "Just look at me. And look at my dress!" Running her hands over the front, smearing more dark powdery ash all over the material, all she could do was stand there with her mouth open.

"What happened to you?" Thelma looked stunned as she came into the store.

"I—I started to light the stove, and all this smoke poured out." Elma swiped the back of her hand over her mouth. "Then, after I put out the fire, I took the pipe off and this fell out." Holding up the bird's nest and motioning to her dress, she grimaced. "You can see what happened next."

Thelma snickered; then her face sobered. "You'd better go back to the house, change out of that dress, and get washed up. While you're gone, I'll clean up in here. Hopefully I'll have it done by the time you get back."

"Danki, Thelma. I'll be back as soon as possible."

When Elma returned to the store half an hour later, she was surprised to see Thelma standing behind the counter, smiling. "Surprise! It's all done." Thelma pointed to the stove. Not only had Thelma cleaned up the mess, but she had the stovepipe back on and a cozy fire going. "It should warm up quickly now."

Elma smiled. "Danki. You're such a big help."

"By the way, what did you do with your dress?" Thelma asked.

Elma sighed. "It's soaking in a bucket of water in the utility room. I'm not sure if that poor dress will ever be the same; it's such a mess. I may replace it with the new dress I still haven't made. Of course," she quickly added, "I have other work dresses I can wear."

"That's true, and at least this all happened when there were no customers in the store. That could have been quite embarrassing."

"You're right." Elma couldn't help giggling. She could only imagine how silly she must have looked, standing there with soot all over her while holding a bird's nest.

"Guess we'd better get busy," Thelma said.

Elma picked up a tablet, preparing to write down whatever needed to be ordered. She'd only made it to the first aisle, when Thelma came by. "I forgot to tell you. When I went to the phone shack I saw someone across the street looking at the house that's for sale."

"Are they Amish or English?"

"Amish. I saw them walking around the yard, and I noticed that the woman's skirt is pleated." Thelma's forehead wrinkled. "I don't think I've ever seen an Amish woman's dress with pleats."

"She's probably from the Graybill area," Elma said. "Didn't someone tell us that many of the Amish women who live there wear skirts like that?"

Thelma tipped her head. "I can't remember. . .maybe." She frowned, brushing at some stray cat hairs on her sweater. "Tiger can sure shed. Guess when I find the time I'll have to brush him again."

"That may help some, but it'll be a constant chore. One more reason I don't like having cats indoors."

Thelma shrugged. "Anyway, it will be nice if we get

new neighbors soon. I'll be anxious to get acquainted."

"You'll have plenty of time for that if they buy the house."

"That's true."

"By the way, were there any important messages?" Elma asked.

"Not a one." Thelma snapped her fingers. "Guess I should have checked for mail when I went to the phone shack. I'll do that now."

Thelma was almost to the mailbox when she noticed Mary Lambright riding past on her bike. Her little boy Richard was in a child's seat on the back. Thelma hollered a greeting to them and waved. Mary and Richard waved back. It had quit raining, but the roads were slightly wet.

Smiling, Thelma stepped up to the box. She was about to reach inside, when she heard a horn honk, followed by the spine-tingling sound of brakes squealing—then a bloodcurdling scream. Thelma rushed out and looked up the road. Mary and Richard lay sprawled on the ground, next to the bike. With her heart in her throat, Thelma dashed to the accident. *Please, God, let them be all right.*

Chapter 9

Thelma dropped to her knees beside Mary and Richard. The driver of the car, a young woman, got out and rushed over. "Oh my! Are either of you hurt?" The woman's voice trembled as she knelt next to Thelma.

"I'm all right—just a few scrapes on my knees and hands," Mary said. "But I'm worried about my little boy." She gestured to Richard, still strapped in his seat at the back of her bike, sobbing and holding his gravel-embedded arm.

"This was my fault," the woman said. "I shouldn't have honked the horn when I saw your bike."

Thelma winced when she saw the way Richard's arm was twisted. "I think his arm is broken," she whispered to Mary. "We have to get him out of that seat. You'll need to take him to the medical clinic and have it X-rayed."

Mary's fingers trembled as she struggled with the safety strap.

"Here, let me try," Thelma offered.

"We can cut the strap with the scissors I have in my purse," the English woman said. "I can call 911 or drive you there. I'll call my boss and let him know I'm gonna be late for work."

Mary nodded. "I'd appreciate the scissors—and a ride to the clinic."

Thelma cut the strap away, and Mary took her son out of the seat. Gathering her son carefully into her arms, Mary said, "It'll be okay, son. The doctor will take good care of you."

While the young woman made the phone call, Thelma

held Richard, and Mary climbed into the backseat of the car. Then Thelma gingerly handed the boy to his mother. It was hard seeing the little tyke grimace in pain.

"I'll take your bike to my place, and someone from your family can pick it up later on." Thelma spoke in a reassuring tone.

Tears gathered in Mary's eyes. "Danki, Elma. My husband, Dan, is at work right now, and my *mamm*'s home with our other son, Philip. It probably won't be till sometime this evening that Dan can come by with our market wagon to pick up my bike."

Thelma was on the verge of correcting Mary, but right now it didn't matter that the woman had mixed her up with Elma. She was used to that. Even some people back home who had known them for years couldn't tell the twins apart. The only thing that mattered was getting Richard's arm looked at. "This evening will be fine. Mary, if you'll give me your address, I'll go to your house and let your mamm know what's happened so she doesn't worry because you haven't returned home."

"That would be most appreciated." Mary's voice was full of emotion.

Thelma gave Mary's arm a tender squeeze. "I'll be praying for Richard."

"Danki." Mary dabbed at the tears on her pale cheeks; then she reached into her purse and took out a notepad and pen. After she wrote down the address, she tore off a piece of paper and handed it to Thelma. "Please tell my mamm not to worry but to pray that Richard's arm does not have a serious break."

"I will," Thelma promised. "And I'll be praying myself."

Elma peered out the front window of the store, wondering where Thelma was. She'd been gone a lot longer than necessary to get the mail. *I wonder if my sister got sidetracked again.* She opened the door and stuck her head out but saw no sign of Thelma in the yard or down the driveway. If Elma hadn't been concerned that a customer could show up, she would have walked out to the mailbox to see if her sister was still there.

I'll give her a few more minutes, she decided, *but if she doesn't show up soon I'll put the CLOSED sign in the window and see if I can find her.*

Elma went back to inventorying the shelves and was about to start on the next row of kitchen items when the front door opened and Thelma rushed in.

"You'll never believe what happened out there," she panted.

"What is it?" Elma asked. "You look *umgerrent.*"

"I am upset. Mary Lambright was on her bicycle with her son Richard on the seat behind her, and. . ." Thelma paused to take a breath. "A car almost hit her, and she and Richard fell off the bike." She moved over to stand beside the woodstove.

"Oh dear," Elma gasped. "Were either of them hurt?"

"Mary was scraped up, and it looked like the little boy's arm was broken. The driver of the car is taking them to the medical clinic. I brought Mary's bike back here. Her husband will pick it up later. Oh, and Mary gave me her address, so I promised to go over to her house and let her mamm know what happened. She's there with Mary's other son, Philip." Thelma was talking so fast Elma could hardly keep up with her.

"I'm sorry to hear about the accident but grateful that it wasn't any worse." Elma thought about her grandparents' fatality. Whether riding in a buggy, on a bicycle, or walking, there was always the danger of being hit by a car.

"I know, but even though the little guy's injuries weren't life threatening, he was frightened and obviously in pain." Thelma fiddled with the paper she held.

"I imagine he would be. Remember when we were eight and I fell from the loft in Dad's barn and broke my *gnechel*? That hurt."

Thelma nodded. "We were all glad it was only your ankle that was broken. You could have been killed, falling a distance like that."

"God watched out for me that day. There's no doubt about it."

Thelma glanced around. "How are things here? Have you gotten much inventory done?"

"Some, but I still have several more shelves to get to, not to mention all the things that are in the store's basement."

"Have you had any customers yet?"

Elma shook her head. "Maybe it's going to be a slow day and we can spend it taking stock of all the things we need to order."

"I know one thing. . . The buggy could use a little cleaning, outside and in. With the rain we've gotten, plus the dust in the air, our rig is looking a bit neglected."

"You're right," Elma agreed. "That's one more thing I'll need to add to my list."

Moving away from the stove, Thelma said, "Since there are no customers at the moment, I'd better head over to Mary's house and let her mamm know what happened."

"Does Mary live far from here?" Elma asked.

"From the address she gave me, I'd say it's about a mile or so."

"That shouldn't take you too long, if you go on your bike."

Thelma paused and shifted her weight from one foot to the other. "Actually, I thought I'd take the horse and buggy and make a stop at the hardware store in town."

Elma's forehead wrinkled. "How come?"

"Remember that paint I forgot to get in Shipshe last week?"

"Jah."

"If I don't get it now, we'll never have the kitchen painted before Mom and Dad get here."

Elma pursed her lips. "You're right about that. Guess

I can get by awhile longer without your help."

"There's one more errand I'll need to run," Thelma said.

"What's that?"

"Before I came back to the store, I checked phone messages again. There was a new one from the people who own the meat locker in town." Thelma grimaced. "They said Grandpa and Grandma's bill hadn't been paid for this month. They asked whether we want to pay it or come by and get what's left in the locker they'd rented."

Elma groaned. "Oh great. I wonder what that will cost. Will it never end?"

Thelma shrugged, turning her hands palms up. "Guess I could go by there and clear out their locker, but I'm not sure how much there is. We may not have room for all of it in the small freezer section of our refrigerator, but we'll slip in whatever we can. Maybe we can precook part of the meat to have for some of the meals we'll be fixing this week."

"You're right," Elma agreed. "Did they say how much the rent would be for the next month?"

"Jah. It's twenty-two dollars. Can we afford that right now?"

"I guess we'll have to." Elma went to the battery-operated cash register behind the counter and took out a twenty dollar bill, plus two ones. "Here you go."

"I'll need some money for the paint too," Thelma reminded.

"Oh, that's right." She handed Thelma another fifty dollars. "I hope this will be enough. If it's not, then get one gallon for now."

"Okay. I'd better get going then." Thelma turned toward the door, glancing at the sky. "Maybe I'll take an umbrella. It was clearing up a little while ago, but I see a few more dark clouds." She slipped on her outer bonnet and grabbed the umbrella.

Elma touched her arm. "Are you sure you want to take Rusty?"

"It's the only way I can take the buggy, and there's

no way I'm going to ride my bike that far, not to mention needing a place to put the paint." Thelma paused. "I'll probably bring home some meat from the locker too. Anyway, Rusty needs to earn his keep around here. He should be worked as much as possible. Otherwise, he may get worse, and I won't let him do that. Dad would want us to hang in there and keep showing Rusty who's boss. Right, Sister?"

Elma hesitated then nodded. "Okay, see you later then."

"I'll be back as soon as I can."

When Thelma went out the door, Elma leaned against the counter and sighed. "I hope I gave Thelma enough money. Even more than that, I hope and pray the horse behaves."

Chapter 10

When Thelma left Mary's house, after notifying Richard's grandmother that he had broken his arm, she headed toward town. She felt a little nervous when she halted Rusty at the first stop sign and he started tossing his head from side to side.

"Calm down," Thelma said soothingly. "We can't go till it's safe." Once she was sure no cars were coming, she guided the horse to make a right-hand turn onto the highway that would take them to the stores in Topeka. Rusty moved at a pretty good clip, but as long as he wasn't running out of control, she didn't mind. The quicker she got to town, the quicker she'd get back to the store to help Elma. At least the trip to the local hardware store wouldn't be as long as it would have been if she'd gone all the way to Shipshewana.

The clouds that had looked threatening when she'd first left home were now breaking apart, letting peeks of sunshine through. Thelma was glad it had quit raining. That made it easier to see, and with less water on the pavement, Rusty was not as likely to spook.

As she drew closer to town, Thelma thought about Richard and wondered how things were going at the clinic. Had he seen the doctor yet? If his arm was broken, would they be able to take care of it there, or would Mary have to take her son to the closest hospital?

If it doesn't take too long at the hardware store and frozen food locker, maybe I'll stop by the clinic before I go home,

Thelma thought. *That way, I'll know for sure what happened to Mary's little boy.*

Joseph had spent the last few hours in Topeka, visiting with the Amish man who owned the harness shop. The man had more business than he could handle and wondered if he could send some customers to Joseph. Never one to turn down a job opportunity, Joseph had eagerly agreed.

Guess I won't need to stop by the office for The Connection *magazine to run an ad like I'd planned,* Joseph thought as he left the harness shop. *Maybe another time, if business gets slow.*

Thinking he ought to make a quick stop at the hardware store to pick up some paint for his bedroom, Joseph directed his horse and buggy in that direction. The horse, which had been moving along steadily, suddenly broke into a canter. "Whoa, boy! Slow down!" Joseph pulled on the reins.

The horse slowed, and in no time, Joseph had the animal under control.

When he entered the hardware store a short time later, he noticed a young Amish woman standing near the aisle where the paint was kept, tapping her chin as she studied the cans.

When he approached, she looked up at him and smiled, revealing a small dimple in her right cheek. "Do you know much about paint?" she asked.

He shrugged. "A l–little." *Oh great. Don't start stuttering now.* Tripping over his words was something Joseph did only when he felt nervous, and for some reason that's how he felt at the moment. The dumb thing was he didn't even know why. He'd never met this woman with the pretty blue eyes before and might never see her again. Besides, a woman as attractive as her was probably married.

"The wording is so small; I'm having a hard time

reading the instructions and recommendations on the paint cans. Would you be able to tell me what kind of paint would be best to use in a kitchen?"

"Umm. . ." Joseph cleared his throat and swallowed. He hoped he wasn't going to stutter again. "I'd say a latex/enamel would be a good choice." *Whew. So far, so good.* Joseph pointed to one of the cans. "What color do you want?"

She pursed her lips while studying the various colors available. "I've been looking at these color samples. I'm thinking an off-white would be best."

He gave a nod. "Makes sense to me."

"I appreciate the advice." She smiled, picked up two cans of paint, and headed to the checkout counter.

"Good luck with your project." Joseph gave her one last glance and moved on to pick out his paint.

When Thelma started for the door, carrying the paint she'd purchased, she caught sight of a flyer taped to the inside of the store window. It was the same as the one she'd picked up in Shipshewana, telling about the upcoming cooking show. She felt certain it was something Elma would want to do with her. After all, who wouldn't want to help a good cause such as this? *Think I'll call the phone number on the flyer and let the person in charge know that my sister and I would like to make something to be auctioned off. I also have one other important call to make.*

She'd barely stepped outside when the red-haired Amish man she'd spoken to about the paint came out the door holding a paintbrush. He approached her in a shy manner, and with a little stutter in his voice, he said, "I—I think this is yours. It was left on the c—counter inside."

Thelma's cheeks warmed as she took the paintbrush from him. "Guess I was in such a hurry, I forgot." For some strange reason it was all she could do to keep from tripping over her own words. Forcing herself to look away from his steady gaze, Thelma glanced to her left. She was stunned to see Rusty prancing up the street, pulling her buggy. "Oh my!" She pointed in that direction. "That's my horse and buggy, with no driver. I must not have tied him securely enough."

The redheaded man sprang into action. As he dashed up the street, his straw hat blew off, landing on the pavement, but he kept running and never looked back. Another Amish man who sported a full beard and had been standing nearby joined the chase as well. With her heart beating wildly, all Thelma could do was stand there, powerless, and watch. What a day full of mishaps this had turned out to be.

By some miracle, the two men managed to get hold of Rusty. Several minutes later, they brought him back to Thelma. She breathed a sigh of relief. Never in a million years had she expected that her and Elma's move to Topeka would bring so much drama.

"Danki," she told the men. "I fear that unpredictable horse would have run into the next county if you two hadn't caught him when you did."

"I'm glad I could help," the older of the two men said, still trying to catch his breath.

The man with red hair gave a nod. "He gave us quite a chase."

Thelma couldn't help but notice how the man's freckles stood out against his rosy cheeks. Despite the fact that his ears stuck out a bit, she thought he was rather good looking. Not in a dashing sort of way, like the blond-haired man she'd bumped heads with at Yoder's Hardware last week, but in a boyish sort of way she found appealing. She knew he wasn't married because he was clean shaven. *Stop thinking such crazy thoughts,* Thelma reprimanded herself. *My focus should be on all that Elma and I need to get done before Mom and Dad arrive, not thinking about men I don't even know.*

"Would one of you mind holding my horse awhile

longer, so I can get the paint and brush put in the buggy?" Thelma asked the men.

"I'd be happy to do that," the bearded man spoke up.

After giving the horse's nose a gentle pat, the younger man with red hair stepped away from Rusty. "I'm glad everything's under control, so I'll be on my way." He gave Thelma a quick nod and hurried off down the street.

Thelma put her purchases on the floor of the passenger's side then stepped into the driver's seat. Gathering up the reins, she waved at the bearded Amish man and headed down the street in the direction of the building where her grandparents had rented a freezer. "Okay, Rusty, you've had your fun for the day. Now you'd better be good."

Fortunately, Rusty behaved himself, and in no time Thelma was guiding the horse up to the hitching rail. She made sure he was securely tied and hurried inside the building. After paying for this month's rent, she removed a few packages of meat from the freezer and placed them in a cooler in the back of her buggy. The meat would come in handy when their parents were here next week. Thelma and Elma would be able to make a variety of dishes with the ground beef. She'd also brought a roast, some stew meat, a couple of steaks, and some breakfast sausage. *If we need any more meat while Mom and Dad are here, at least it's not far to go to get more.*

From there, Thelma headed to the clinic, where she found Mary sitting in the waiting room. "How's Richard?" Thelma asked, taking a seat beside Mary.

"His arm is broken," Mary replied. "The doctor is putting the cast on now. I came out here to call my driver for a ride home."

"Have you already done that? If not, I could take you."

Mary smiled. "I appreciate the offer, but Carolyn is already on the way."

"Oh, okay." Thelma glanced at the clock on the far wall. As much as she would like to stay until Richard came out, she'd been gone over two hours and knew she really should get home. "I'll try to stop by your place sometime tomorrow to see how Richard is doing," she told Mary.

Mary nodded. "That'd be nice. I'm sure he'd like that."

"See you tomorrow then." Thelma gave Mary's arm a gentle squeeze and headed out the door.

By the time Thelma guided Rusty off the road and onto their driveway, she was more than ready to get out. She'd struggled to keep him under control the whole way home. She wondered how long it would be before he settled down and became easier to deal with. Pearl, their horse back home, had never been this testy. From the day she and Elma had first gotten the gentle mare, she'd always been easy to handle.

Remembering the phone calls she wanted to make, Thelma stopped the horse outside the phone shack and secured him to a post. She stepped into the small building and dialed the first number. After she'd made both calls, she untied the horse and hopped back into the buggy. As she directed Rusty up the driveway toward the barn, Thelma noticed three buggies parked outside the store. *Oh great. I wonder how many customers there are and how long they've been here. I'll bet Elma is upset with me for being gone so long and leaving her here to run things by herself.*

Thelma jumped out of the buggy and quickly took care of Rusty. Once she'd put him in the corral, she grabbed the cooler of meat and took it to the house to put in the refrigerator. She would get the paint out of the buggy later.

Standing in the kitchen, staring at the basement door, Thelma was tempted to make a quick trip down to check on Misty and her babies but figured it was best to get right over to the store. Still, she paused to listen and was satisfied that all was quiet.

In addition to helping Elma wait on customers,

Thelma was anxious to tell her sister what she'd found out about Mary's son. It would be best not to say anything about Rusty taking off when she was in town. And she wouldn't bother to mention how skittish he'd acted on the way home. No point making Elma more afraid of the horse than she already was. And Thelma would certainly not tell her sister about one of the phone calls she'd made.

Chapter 11

"I can't believe Mom and Dad will be here this evening," Elma told Thelma as they cleaned the kitchen floor and counters.

"I know," Thelma agreed, "and I'm glad we managed to get the kitchen painted before they arrive. How exciting it will be to have them here. They'll be the first guests to stay with us as new owners of this house." Her bubbly words bounced off the walls. "Hey Sister, we can have them sign the guest book when they arrive. There'll be all new memories to make while they're here." She pushed the soapy mop around the kitchen floor.

"We've worked so hard getting ready for their arrival, yet there's still so much to be done." Elma sighed, pinning a wayward strand of hair back under her headscarf. "I think every bone in my body aches."

"Mine too." Thelma set the mop aside, rubbing her neck. "I'm glad we decided to close the store today so we could take care of any last-minute things that needed to be done here at the house." She smiled. "And I'm glad I went over to see how little Richard was doing last week, because there hasn't been time this week, with all we've needed to do."

"I keep forgetting to ask. Did he like the book and candy you took him?"

Thelma nodded. "He especially liked *The Wisdom of Solomon* because it's a picture book, so he can look at the drawings and know what's happening in the story, even though he can't read yet."

"That's nice." Elma gestured to the stove. "Have you thought about what we could fix for supper this evening? I'm sure Mom and Dad will be here before it's time to eat."

"I thought maybe we could fix some savory stew. There's a recipe for it in one of Grandma's cookbooks, and we have some stew meat I brought home last week from the freezer they rented. I put it, along with the rest of the meat, in the smaller freezer compartment of our refrigerator. If I get it out now, I don't think it'll take long to thaw."

"That's a good idea." Elma put her cleaning supplies away. "While you get the meat, I'll cut some vegetables for the stew."

"Don't you want to wait till the meat has thawed?"

Elma shook her head. "It'll save time if I do it now. Once I get the veggies cut, I'll refrigerate them until it's time to start the stew."

"Guess that makes sense." Thelma took the package of meat from the freezer and placed it in a bowl of cool water. "Think I'll go to the basement and do a little more cleaning down there before it's time to start lunch."

Elma tipped her head. "I don't think Mom and Dad will be doing much in the basement while they're here, so that's not really a priority right now."

"Mom may go down to wash clothes, and I want Dad to look at the water tank," Thelma replied. "Sure don't want them walking through cobwebs or getting their clothes dusty."

Elma shrugged. "You're right."

When Thelma left the kitchen, Elma took out some carrots, celery, potatoes, and onions and placed them on the counter beside the cutting board. As she washed the vegetables in the sink, she thought about her sister and the strange way she'd been acting for the past week. For some reason, Thelma kept making unnecessary trips to the basement. At least Elma saw them as unnecessary. It was one thing to go down there to wash clothes, but Thelma had already done so much cleaning downstairs that the place had to be spick-and-span by now. *And why, every time I say I'm going to the basement, does she offer to go in my place?*

After Thelma fed Misty and filled her bowl with fresh water, she knelt beside the box and petted the kittens. They were so cute and soft. One kitten was gray like its mother, one was all white, and two resembled a black barn cat Thelma had named Shadow. No doubt, he was the father. Thelma felt guilty for keeping the cats a secret, and she didn't know how much longer she could prevent Elma from coming down to the basement. The one thing she had on her side was that her sister had so many other things to keep her busy.

In addition to trying to get things organized at the store, both she and Elma had spent some time each evening going through some of their grandparents' things. They'd decided to put some of Grandpa's marbles in one of Grandma's old canning jars Thelma had found in the basement. She'd placed it in the middle of the kitchen table as a centerpiece. To some, it may look ordinary, but to Thelma it was a sentimental reminder of her grandparents. She was sure that Elma felt the same. It was fun to look at the variety of marbles in different sizes. Some were clear, some were solid colors, and other marbles had a pattern inside. Since Grandpa had collected so many marbles, she and her sister decided to put the rest of them in glass jars and try to sell them at the store. In the hall closet upstairs, among the other linens, they'd found a box of beautiful pillowcases Grandma had embroidered. They looked as if they'd never been used. Each set had been beautifully wrapped in white tissue paper and neatly folded in the box. Because there were too many for the twins to use, they would ask Mom if she'd like to have a couple of sets. The rest of the pillowcases they would sell.

I can't worry about that now, she told herself. *I have to get back upstairs and see what else needs to be done.* Thelma grabbed the little garbage can and emptied the contents into a small cardboard box. Still holding on to the box, she knelt down and took one last look at the kittens. After scratching Misty behind the ears, Thelma rose to her feet, turned off the gas lamps, and headed upstairs.

"How are things going with the stew?" Thelma asked later that afternoon. "Do you think it'll be done before our folks get here?"

Elma lifted the kettle lid and pierced a piece of carrot with a fork. "The vegetables are tender. Think I'll move the kettle to the back of the stove so the stew will stay warm but won't keep cooking. Otherwise, everything will turn to mush." She glanced at the clock. "It's four thirty. I wish we knew exactly what time to expect them, because there's no point baking the biscuits until we see—"

"The whites of their eyes," Thelma finished Elma's sentence and giggled. "I've always thought that saying was kind of *schpassich.*"

Elma snickered. "It is rather funny."

At the sound of a vehicle coming up the driveway, the twins both looked out the window. "It's Mom and Dad. I recognize their driver's van." Elma clutched her sister's hand. "Is that a horse trailer the van is pulling?"

"It looks like it to me." Taking Elma's hand, Thelma opened the door.

By the time the twins stepped outside, their parents had gotten out of the van. "It's so good to see you!" Thelma and Elma said simultaneously as they hugged Mom and Dad.

"It's good to see you too," their folks agreed.

"I have a surprise for you," Dad said as he and his driver, Dave Henderson, went to the back of the van. A few minutes later, Dad came back, leading a dark gray mare. "Look who missed you," he said with a big grin.

"It's Pearl!" Elma was so excited to see their own horse that her tears started to flow. "What made you bring Pearl with you? Not that I mind—I'm thrilled."

Dad motioned to Thelma. "Your sister had something to do with it, but I'll let her explain."

While gently stroking Pearl's neck, as the mare

nuzzled her hand, Elma looked over at Thelma.

Her sister smiled. "I called Dad a week ago and told him about Rusty's antics. Since I've been worried about you having to drive that unpredictable horse, I asked if Dad would bring Pearl."

"Oh Sister, I'm so glad you did this for me." Elma's eyes revealed the depth of her emotions.

"It wasn't all me. Mom and Dad did the biggest part in making this happen," Thelma said.

Full of gratitude, Elma gave Thelma a hug, and then she embraced her parents again. "Danki to all of you for being so thoughtful and thinking of me." In addition to having missed the docile mare she and Thelma had shared for the last seven years, she would feel a lot safer driving this horse. Her sister and parents had lifted a huge weight from Elma's shoulders. There would be plenty of room for Pearl in Cutter's old stall. Maybe now Thelma would be willing to sell Rusty. But she would wait to bring that subject up some other time. Right now, all Elma wanted to do was spend time with her folks.

That evening, as they sat around the kitchen table eating supper, Thelma felt a sense of satisfaction. Not only had she surprised her sister by seeing that their horse had been brought here, but they had a whole week to visit with Mom and Dad.

"This stew sure is tasty," Dad smacked his lips. "Whoever made it did a fine job."

"I can't take the credit," Thelma spoke up. "Elma did most of the work on the stew. All I really did was take out the meat to thaw." She cringed, motioning to the overly brown biscuits. "I was responsible for those, but I think that old woodstove's oven is more to blame for them getting too brown."

"Maybe the thermometer isn't working," Mom said. "You may need to buy a new one."

"Do you think it's as simple as that?" Elma asked with a hopeful expression.

Mom nodded. "When I was young, my mamm had a woodstove in her kitchen, and I had to learn to cook on it."

"Really? You never told us that before," Thelma said.

Mom smiled and patted Thelma's hand. "Maybe tomorrow we'll make a batch of chocolate chip cookies."

"While you ladies are doing that, I'll see about fixing the leak I discovered under the kitchen sink," Dad said.

Elma's cheeks turned pink. "You know about that?"

He gave a nod. "In addition to the odor of mildew, when I pulled the curtain back to look under the sink for some hand cleaner awhile ago, I saw the tape you have wrapped around the pipe." He jiggled his eyebrows playfully. "Masking tape doesn't hold up too well when there's a leak."

Elma looked at Thelma and rolled her eyes. "Is that what you wrapped the pipe with?"

Feeling rather foolish, Thelma could only nod.

"It's okay," Dad reassured her. "I will not only see that the pipe is fixed, but I'll repair the hole in the floor beneath it."

Mom's eyebrows shot up. "There's a hole in the floor? Oh Jacob, this old house must be falling apart." She pointed to the missing handles on a few of the cupboards. "And those aren't the only things that need fixing. When we stepped onto the porch to come inside this afternoon, I felt like I might fall through one of those squeaky boards."

"Actually, we've started making lists of things we've found that need to be fixed or replaced," Elma explained. "Unfortunately, our lists keep growing, and we've only been here two weeks."

"The place does need some fixing up, but I'm sure that it has a few good years left." Dad looked over at the twins and winked. "I won't be able to fix everything for you, but I'll get as much done as I can while your mamm and I are here—the most important things, at least."

"Danki, Dad. We appreciate that," the twins both said.

I wonder if I should tell Dad about the hot water tank

right now, Thelma thought. *Guess I'll wait until later this evening to say anything. If I bring it up now, Mom will probably get upset. I can see by her expression and the tone of her voice that she thinks we made a mistake trying to take over this place. Well, we're determined to make a go of it, and nothing she can say will change our minds.* Thelma glanced at her sister. *At least I hope Elma's not having any second thoughts.*

Chapter 12

Kathryn shivered as she stepped out of the bathroom and into the bedroom next door. "Did you have any hot water when you took a shower?" she asked her husband.

Jacob shook his head. "I wouldn't say it was hot. More like lukewarm."

She rubbed her hands over her arms. "Mine was slightly warm for a few minutes, but then it turned cold. There must be something wrong with the water tank."

"I'll go down to the basement and take a look at it in the morning," he said. "We had a long day traveling and stayed up late visiting with the twins. It's time for you and me to go to bed."

Kathryn yawned, turning back the covers. "You're right. Tomorrow will be a busy day, and we need to be well rested. Those girls of ours need all the help they can get. While we're here, I want to help out as much as possible."

"Same here. I noticed that there's a lot of outside work to be done."

"I wish we could be with the twins longer than a week." Her brows furrowed. "I'm worried about them, Jacob. They took on a huge task when they moved here, and to do it all by themselves, well, I think it's way too much. If they had husbands it wouldn't be so bad, but at the rate things are going, it doesn't look like either of them will ever get married."

"Never say never." Jacob placed his hands gently

on her shoulders. "You worry too much, Kathryn. If the good Lord wants our daughters to have mates, then it will happen in His time. And as far as them taking on the job of running my folks' store and keeping up with this place. . .I think they're up to the challenge. They made it through two weeks. Even with all they've found wrong so far, it sounds like they're determined to make it work. We should be pleased to have daughters who don't give up so easily." He bent his head and kissed Kathryn's cheek. "Now let's go to bed and try to get a good night's sleep." Jacob waited for her to climb into bed before he turned off the gas lamp.

Kathryn drew in a deep breath and released it slowly. *Jacob may think the twins are up to the challenge, but I'm their mother, and I could tell the minute we got here that they're both exhausted. If I have anything to say about it, Thelma and Elma will be home before Christmas.*

"Are you girls having trouble with your water tank?" Dad asked the following morning during breakfast. "Your mamm had a cold shower last night."

Thelma gulped. Last night she'd planned to ask Dad to take a look at it but had gotten so caught up in visiting and completely forgot. "I know, and I'm sorry about that, Mom." She handed Dad a fresh cup of coffee. "It's not heating like it should. The other day I noticed a puddle of water in the basement near the tank."

"Really?" Elma turned from the stove, where she was frying sausage. "How come you never mentioned it to me?"

"You knew about the cold showers," Thelma reminded.

"Jah, but this is the first I've heard about water on the basement floor." Elma frowned.

"I only saw it one time and figured it could have been from something else."

"I'll go down and take a look as soon as breakfast is over." Dad reached over and tapped Elma's arm as she set the pan of breakfast sausage on a pot holder in the middle of the table.

"I'll go with you," Thelma was quick to say. She still hadn't told Elma about Misty and the kittens. She sure didn't want her finding out about them today. With Mom here, she'd probably side with Elma, and the kittens would have to be taken out to the barn. Ever since the twins were little, it seemed like Mom sided more with Elma on things than she did Thelma. It wasn't that she loved Elma more; they just had similar likes and dislikes.

Wanting to change the subject, Thelma brought up the box of pillowcases they'd found in the upstairs closet.

"That's right." Elma glanced at Mom and Dad before starting to fry some eggs to go with the sausage. "We found this box of beautiful pillowcases Grandma must have embroidered. They look like they've never been used."

"There are several sets of them, and we'll keep a few," Thelma added. "But before we sell any of them in the store, we thought maybe you and Mom would like to have some, since your mamm embroidered them." She brought over a plate of toast and handed it to Dad.

Before Dad could respond, Mom said, "I would think about that before you decide to sell any of them. Your daed and I could use some new pillowcases, so I may take a few sets. Why don't you and Elma keep the rest? You could regret it later on if you sell them."

"Mom may be right," Elma said while using a spatula to put an egg on each of their plates. "Maybe we should keep all of the pillowcases—in case we ever get married."

Thelma nodded. "She did do a beautiful job on them, and who knows, we may have a use for them sometime in the future."

Thelma and Elma pulled out chairs and sat down at the same time. "I'm glad we talked about this," Elma said. "Sometimes I'm too quick to get rid of things; then later, I regret my decision."

"I think we've all done that at one time or another,"

Dad commented; then he bowed his head. "Let's pray."

When the prayers ended, they visited some more. Thelma was in a good mood, happy that she hadn't burned the toast. But all too soon, the joy of the moment was gone when Mom, who had poured herself a glass of orange juice, let out an ear-piercing scream. "Ach, there's a *gross maus* eating the bread we left on the counter!"

All heads turned in the direction she was pointing. "That's not a big mouse," Dad said, his eyes widening. "It's a *ratt*!"

"A rat?" Mom and Elma shouted in unison. Faces pale, they both jumped on their chairs, jarring the kitchen table. Mom's orange juice spilled, and Elma's fork flew off her plate and clanked on the floor.

Thelma groaned. It was bad enough that they'd had some mice in their house. Now this?

"I'll take care of that unwanted creature!" Dad leaped out of his chair, grabbed a broom from the utility room, and rushed back to the kitchen. By the time he came in, however, the rat had dived to the floor.

Fearful that it would run under the table, Thelma lifted her feet. Dad swung the broom, but the rat was too fast. It quickly disappeared under the curtain beneath the kitchen sink. Dad jerked the material open, but the rat, thumping its tail, made its escape through the hole in the floor.

"Oh great." Mom pressed her hand to her forehead and moaned. "As if things aren't bad enough around here already, now the girls have a *ratt* in their home."

"Calm down, Kathryn." Dad held up his hand. "I'll hitch Pearl to the twins' buggy and go to the hardware store today. I'm sure I can buy a rat trap there. Better yet, I'll take Rusty. From what Thelma said when she called us the other day, it sounds like that spunky horse could use some more time on the road." He chuckled, looking over at Mom. "So far there hasn't been a dull moment around this place."

"Then we. . .we'd better all go." Mom's voice trembled as she continued to stand on her chair. "Because I'm certainly not going to stay here with a rat!"

"Before anything else, I'll throw out that bread. Also, I'd better use some disinfectant wipes on the whole counter. Who knows where that dirty rat has been?" Elma picked up the bread bag and tossed it into the garbage can. "We'd best not leave any more food out unless it's in a sealed container."

"That would be a smart idea," Mom agreed. "Besides, who knows what kind of diseases that thing may be carrying around? I hope we can catch it before we leave for home."

Dad gave a nod. "Not to worry. I'm sure we'll get that rat caught in no time at all."

"Mom, why don't you come out to the store with me and Thelma?" Elma suggested. "We still have a lot of work to do out there, and we need to be there for at least part of the day because we may get some customers." Glancing at the curtain beneath the sink, she lowered herself into her chair.

Mom nodded and sat down as well. "That's a good idea. I'd be happy to help with whatever needs to be done in the store."

"Would you two mind if I go with Dad after I get the counter cleaned?" Thelma asked, looking at Elma and then their mother.

"That's fine with me," Elma said with a nod.

Dad put the broom away and took a seat at the table. "Before we go anywhere, I'm going to finish my breakfast. Then I'll see about closing up that hole in the floor under the sink. After that, I'll head down to the basement and take a look at the water tank."

"Did Grandma and Grandpa have rats to deal with?" Thelma asked.

Dad shrugged. "I don't know. If they did, they never said anything about it to me. Maybe with their house

92

sitting empty for a few weeks after their death, the mice and rat moved in."

Elma frowned. "They can't move out soon enough to suit me."

While Elma helped Mom do the breakfast dishes, she kept glancing down, fearful that the rat might make another appearance, even though Dad had put a temporary patch of wood over the hole before he and Thelma went downstairs. She couldn't believe all the problems she and her sister had encountered since they'd moved to Topeka. Was there no end in sight? How glad she was that the rat had appeared when Dad was here. She had every confidence that he would get rid of it too. Elma knew the unwanted creature had made its escape and disappeared down the hole in the kitchen floor. But the route it took would put it somewhere in the basement. She hoped her sister would keep a watchful eye on her surroundings and be wary of that rat and its creepy long tail.

Mom reached for a dish to dry as she looked over at Elma. "You girls really ought to sell this place and move back home. It's not safe here, and there's too much work."

"I don't think we're in any grave danger," Elma said, "but you're right, there's a lot of work to be done."

"So you'll consider selling?" Mom's expression was hopeful.

Elma shook her head. "Thelma and I both want to make a go of this venture. It's become a challenge for us that we can't back away from. Can you understand that?"

Mom pursed her lips. "Not really, but it's your life and your decision, so I'll try to keep my opinions to myself."

Elma smiled. "We don't mind your opinion on things, but we also need your support."

"You've got it." Mom glanced at the clock. "I wonder what's taking your *daed* and *schweschder* so long. Seems like they've been down in that basement quite a while."

"Should we check on them?" Elma asked.

Mom nodded. "The dishes are done now anyway, so jah, I think we should go downstairs."

"What are you two still doing down here?"

Thelma jumped at the sound of her sister's voice. "Oh, umm. . . Dad was checking the water tank."

"That's true," Dad said, "and I discovered that in addition to the gas burner being shot, the bottom of the tank is rusting out. I'm afraid you're gonna have to get a new one."

Elma's mouth formed an O. "That'll probably be expensive. I don't think we can afford it right now."

"What other choice do we have?" Thelma asked. "We can't keep taking cold showers."

"Not to worry," Dad said. "I'll pay for a new tank. Think I'd better call my driver at the place he's staying in Middlebury and see if he can take me to Goshen to get a new one today." He looked at Thelma. "Instead of going to the hardware store here in Topeka, I can pick up a rat trap while I'm in Goshen. Do you still want to go with me?"

She nodded. "I sure do. And danki, Dad, for offering to get that for us."

"No problem; I'm glad to help out."

Suddenly, Misty appeared, meowing and swishing her tail against Elma's legs.

Elma jumped back. "Ach, what's this katz doing down here?" She eyed Thelma suspiciously. "Did you bring her into the house?"

Thelma shook her head. "Remember that noise I heard last week before we left for church?"

"Jah, but when you came down here you said you couldn't find anything."

"I didn't at first. Not until I came back down again." Thelma moistened her lips with the tip of her tongue. "What I discovered that second time was Misty, and she had given birth to a *bussli*."

Elma blinked. "There's a kitten down here too?"

"Not just one. Misty had more." Thelma held up four

fingers then watched as her mother crouched down to look at the kittens. Gingerly picking one up, she held it close to her chest, petting it carefully.

"Well, they can't stay." Elma shook her head. "The mother cat and her babies need to be out in the barn."

"I disagree," Mom said as she stood. "If you've had mice and now a rat in the house, the logical thing to do is keep some katze around. Look at this cute little thing." She nuzzled the ball of fur against her cheek. "You don't really want to take them to the barn, do you, Elma?"

Dad, who hadn't said a word so far, spoke up. "Your mamm's right, Elma. Having a cat in the house is a good way to keep rodents away."

Thelma was surprised to see her mother cooing over the kitten. And she certainly never expected Mom to side with her on this issue. She was glad Dad was in agreement too.

Elma sighed. "I suppose you're right, but we don't need five katze in here." She gestured to Misty, who had moved over to rub against Thelma's leg.

Thelma bent down to pet the cat; then she too picked up one of the kittens. "As soon as the kittens are old enough to be weaned, I'll see if I can find them all homes. Then we can let either Misty or Tiger come into the house for at least part of each day."

Elma frowned. "I'm not thrilled about the idea, but it looks like I don't have much choice in the matter."

Mom slipped her arm around Elma's waist. "You'll get used to the idea, dear, especially if the katz catches that old ratt."

"I can't wait for that."

Chapter 13

Thelma kept her eyes closed and breathed slowly in and out, trying to make herself relax, but sleep wouldn't come. The last time she'd looked at the clock beside her bed, she'd realized she had been lying in bed for more than an hour. She couldn't stop thinking about the events of the day. Her brain felt like it was going in fast motion. *I hope I can fall asleep soon, or I'll be exhausted in the morning.*

Slowly, she pushed back the covers and went to stand by the window. The moon wasn't full yet, but bright enough to illuminate her room and create shadows in the yard below. Lifting the window a ways, Thelma breathed in the cool night air. The only sound was a lone katydid singing as if it were still August. It was the middle of September, and the weather had been giving little hints of what was soon to follow.

Thelma yawned and rubbed her arms, shivering from the chill. She lowered the window and climbed back into bed. Breathing in deeply, smelling the fresh air that now lingered in her room, she rolled onto her side, hugging her pillow. Closing her eyes, she smiled, thinking how nice it was having Mom and Dad here. It almost made her feel like a child again, with no worries. But she didn't want their visit to be all work like it had been today. While Dad and Thelma were in Goshen, Elma and Mom had worked in the store, cleaning, organizing, and waiting on customers. After Dad and

Thelma came back, Thelma had fixed sandwiches and brought lunch out to the store. When they'd finished eating, Dad set up the water tank. How nice it was to finally have hot water.

The big old rat still hadn't been caught, but Dad had set a trap for it, and they'd let Tiger into the house before going to bed. Hopefully, the long-tailed creepy critter would be gone by morning.

Thelma reflected once again on how Mom had sided with her about having a cat in the house. Poor Elma still wasn't happy about it, but at least she'd accepted the idea. With the fear her sister had over mice and rats, it was a wonder she didn't insist on having several cats around, even if she was afraid of them scratching her. "Give them a wide berth, and they'll leave you alone." That's what Dad had always said about the cats they had at home. Of course, those felines he was referring to stayed outside for the most part.

Before heading to bed, Elma told Thelma that Mom had tried to talk her into moving back home. Thelma had been pleased to hear that her sister told Mom she was committed to making things work here.

As a sense of drowsiness came over her, Thelma pulled the blanket up to her chin and snuggled against her pillow. She'd started to drift off, when a loud clatter, followed by a catlike shriek, brought her straight up. As the noise continued, she leaned forward, realizing that it was coming from somewhere downstairs—the kitchen, perhaps.

Thelma climbed out of bed, put her robe and slippers on, and grabbed a flashlight. She clicked it on, but the beam grew dim. "Oh great! This thing is useless, and I have no batteries up here." Thelma hit the flashlight a few times, hoping it would brighten the beam, but all that did was make the light go completely out, so she dropped it onto her bed. Using the glow of the moon shining through her window, she carefully made her way to the door. Her curiosity about the ruckus downstairs was enough to give her the determination to try and navigate her way down the steps.

When Thelma stepped out of her room, she nearly bumped into Elma outside her bedroom door. "Where's your flashlight, Sister?" Elma whispered.

"Ach my! You startled me. It's on my bed. The batteries must be low because it isn't bright enough to help anyone." Thelma also spoke in a quiet tone.

"Did you hear that noise?" Elma rasped. "What's going on downstairs? It woke me out of a sound sleep."

"I–I'm not sure, but I think we'd better check it out."

"Let me get my flashlight first," Elma said. "We'd probably fall down the steps without some light to guide us."

"Okay. I'll wait right here till you get back."

When Elma returned with her flashlight, she led the way and Thelma followed. "I wonder if all that commotion woke our folks."

"I wouldn't be surprised," Elma responded. "I don't see how anyone could sleep with all that racket."

As Elma led the way with her flashlight, the twins went carefully down the stairs, where they met Mom and Dad, both heading for the kitchen. When they all stepped into the room, and Elma turned on the gas lamp, Thelma gasped. Tiger was on the counter near the sink. The cat's rigid frame moved in closer to his prey, while he growled and hissed. Tiger seemed larger than he was, hunching his back as he swatted and nipped at the rat. The next thing she knew, the fat rodent was in the sink. Like a flash, Tiger jumped in there too. A few seconds later, the cat leaped out of the sink with the rat in his mouth. When Tiger's paws hit the floor, his head jerked forward, and he dropped the rat.

Mom and Elma both screamed as the rat zipped under the table, with the cat in hot pursuit.

"I'll get the broom!" Dad shouted, while Mom and Elma each grabbed hold of a chair and climbed up on the seat.

Unsure of what to do, Thelma stood off to one side so she wouldn't get hit when Dad returned, swinging that broom.

By the time Dad came back, Tiger had caught the rat again, and the rodent was dead.

Thelma breathed a sigh of relief. At least that problem had been solved.

"What are you baking?" Elma asked when she entered the kitchen that Wednesday morning and found Thelma putting something into the oven.

Thelma closed the oven door and smiled when she turned to face Elma. "I mixed a batch of dough for surprise muffins. I put a teaspoon of strawberry jam in the center of each muffin."

"Sounds good. Should I fix some oatmeal to go with them, or would scrambled eggs be better?"

"We have a lot of eggs in the refrigerator, so I think you should scramble some eggs."

"Okay." Elma went to get the eggs. "I'm surprised Mom and Dad aren't up yet. They're usually such early risers."

"I know, but with all the ruckus last night, between the cat and the rat, we were all up later than normal."

Elma took the egg carton over to the counter—a place she'd made sure to clean thoroughly before going to bed last night. Who knew what kind of horrible germs that old rat had left behind, not to mention the cat's dirty paws? "It's hard for me to say this, but I'm glad we let Tiger come into the house last evening. As far as I'm concerned, he can come in every night."

Thelma smiled. "I'm glad we're in agreement on this. Between him being up here, and Misty in the basement, we shouldn't have any more mice or rats to deal with from now on."

Elma wrinkled her nose. "I certainly hope not. Those creatures are ekelhaft."

"I agree. They're downright disgusting." Thelma went to the cupboard and took out four plates. "Guess I'll set the table while the muffins are baking."

"Should I wait to cook the *oier* till Mom and Dad are up?" Elma asked. "I sure wouldn't want to serve them cold eggs."

"That's probably a good idea." Thelma motioned to the teakettle whistling on the stovetop. "Let's have a cup of tea while we're waiting for them."

"That'd be nice." Elma beat the eggs and added some milk, then she set the mixture aside and took a seat at the table, while Thelma fixed their tea.

"Poor Grandma and Grandpa. So much needed to be done around this place. I guess it was too much for them to keep up." Elma blew on her cup of tea. "I wish Mom and Dad didn't have to go home next week. They've been such a big help already, and since there's so much yet to be done, a lot more could be accomplished if they could stay longer."

"You're right," Thelma agreed, "but they have a store to run and need to get back to Sullivan. Plus, I don't want them working the whole time they're here, but it seems that's what they want to do for most of their visit."

"I know, and we can't reject their offer of help. That would hurt their feelings." Elma sighed. "I'm sure going to miss them when they leave."

"Are you feeling homesick?"

"Maybe a little. I was doing fine till Mom and Dad came. Then I started missing the familiarity of home and being with our folks."

Thelma patted Elma's arm. "I'm sure things will be better once we develop some close friendships here. It's not like we can never visit Mom and Dad again. They said they'd try to come here for Christmas, and if they can't, then maybe we can hire a driver and go there."

"What's that smell?" Mom sniffed the air as she entered the room. "Is something burning?"

Thelma jumped up. "Ach, my muffins! I hope they're not

ruined." She dashed across the room, grabbed a pot holder, and flung open the oven door. A puff of smoke billowed out. Thelma groaned while waving the smoke away with the pot holder. "Oh no, they're not fit for any of us to eat!" She set a folded towel on the counter and placed the muffins on that.

Elma grimaced. Even the tops of the muffins were burned.

"Look at it this way," Mom said cheerfully. "The *hinkel* will have something to nibble on."

Elma snickered, but Thelma frowned. "I'm not sure even the chickens would eat these," she muttered, dumping the muffins into a plastic container. "I should have kept an eye on that oven. Now, thanks to me, we won't be eating my surprise muffins."

"It's all right, Sister. It could have happened to me. We'll still have scrambled eggs." Elma pointed to the bowl of eggs she'd mixed up.

"You know what I think you girls need?" Mom moved over to the stove.

"What's that?" they asked.

"A lesson in cooking on an antique woodstove."

"Or maybe," Dad said, entering the kitchen, "what our daughters need is for each of them to find a husband who can cook."

LaGrange

Joseph's hands shook as he fumbled with the harness he was working on. He'd made oatmeal for breakfast and had managed to scorch it, so he'd ended up eating nothing and drinking three cups of coffee instead. Not the best way to begin his day, but with all the work he had facing him, he didn't want to take the time to cook another batch of oatmeal.

"Probably would have ruined that too," he muttered under his breath. He heard a commotion outside and stopped to look out the window. Usually when someone came to visit, his dog, Ginger, alerted him. Grinning, he watched the golden retriever sitting at the base of the oak tree in the yard between his house and shop. With tail wagging, the dog kept her head tipped toward the branches high in the tree.

Glancing up, Joseph saw a big black crow, squawking loudly as it looked down at Ginger. "Crazy critters," Joseph muttered. He tapped on the window. "Knock off the noise, Ginger!"

As the crow flew off and the dog wandered toward the barn, Joseph returned to the table. Normally, Ginger's barking didn't get on his nerves, but today he felt kind of gloomy and a bit lonely too. He had been on his own since he'd bought the small log cabin house and harness shop eight years ago. Even though his folks and sister, Katie, lived in the area, their homes weren't close enough that he could take his meals with them every day. In addition to Joseph's inability to cook, he tended to be a procrastinator, which meant he often put off grocery shopping. That led to the problem of not having enough food in the house, which was the situation he'd been faced with this morning. At first, Joseph had planned to fry some eggs, but when he'd opened the refrigerator, there weren't any eggs. His next choice was cold cereal, but there wasn't any milk.

As Joseph sat holding his cup of coffee, a thought popped into his head. *I think there's a package of cheese and crackers in my other jacket that I wore last week.* Setting his mug on the workbench, he walked over to the coatrack. He put his hand into the pocket, but it came up empty. Joseph checked the other pocket, and this time he pulled out the sealed snack. "Wish this were a hot meal instead of cold crackers," he mumbled, heading back to the bench.

Mom would say I was being too picky. Joseph bent down to pick up a leather strap from the floor. *And if Katie had been in my kitchen this morning, she would have said that I needed to find a good* fraa *who could cook.* He sucked in his bottom lip. *Maybe I do need a wife, but who's gonna want someone with ears that stick out and who can't talk to a woman without stuttering?*

Chapter 14

Topeka

"I can't believe it's time for us to go home." Mom dabbed at the tears on her cheeks. "It seems like we just got here, yet it's been a whole week."

"Jah, and about all we did was work. I wish we had an extra week to sit and visit," Thelma said in a tone of regret.

"Don't worry about that," Mom assured her. "There will be plenty of other times to visit."

"I hope so." Elma shivered as she stood between Mom and Thelma, while Dad put their suitcases in their driver's van. Not only was it four in the morning, but a steady breeze made the air quite chilly. "I feel bad that you wouldn't let us fix you some breakfast before you leave."

"That's okay," Dad called. "We'll be stopping somewhere to eat along the way, and we appreciate the fruit you gave us to snack on."

Elma tried not to cry as she held Mom's hand. "We'll miss you and Dad, and we appreciate all the things you did to help out."

"It was our pleasure." Mom sniffed. "If you need anything, please let us know."

Dad came around from the back of the van and gave each of the twins a hug. Then he reached into his pocket and handed Thelma some cash. "This should give you enough to hire someone to do a few repairs around here. I'd start with that saggy porch, if I were you."

"Danki, Dad," Elma and Thelma said.

"If you need more, let me know." Dad turned to Mom

then. "Are you ready to hit the road, Kathryn?"

"Not really," she said tearfully, "but I know we need to go."

The twins hugged their parents one last time and waved as the van pulled out of the yard.

Elma slipped her arm around Thelma's waist. "We need to get to work, or we'll be blubbering and wiping tears away the rest of the day."

"I agree. It will be easier not to miss them if we keep busy." Thelma sighed. "I sure hope they can come here for Christmas."

"Same here."

Thelma held the money Dad had given her. "Now that Dad gave us this, should we see about hiring someone to do the porch?"

"Jah, but we have so many other things going on right now, I think we should wait on that awhile."

"You mean like canning the rest of the beets you and Mom picked yesterday?"

Elma nodded. "Mom was certainly a big help in the kitchen and out here." She gestured to their weed-free garden.

"I hope we can remember everything she told us about cooking and baking with that old woodstove," Thelma said. "I'm wondering if we should have written it all down."

"You may be right," Elma said as they walked toward the house. "The biscuits I baked last night turned out pretty tasty, thanks to Dad putting in a new stove thermometer."

When they entered the house, Thelma touched Elma's arm and said, "Speaking of baking, I keep forgetting to tell you that I signed us up for the cooking show that takes place the first Saturday of October."

Elma's mouth dropped open. "You did what?"

"I signed us up for the—"

"Without asking me?" Elma could hardly believe her sister would do something like that.

"When I told you about the cooking show, you seemed interested, so I assumed—"

"You should never assume anything." Elma strode into the kitchen and flopped into a chair at the table. "And I think you misunderstood what I said before, which was that I would give it some thought."

"Have you?" Thelma's wide-eyed expression and air of enthusiasm made it hard to say no.

"I don't see how we can bake anything when we haven't truly mastered that old stove." Elma placed her hand above her eyes. "Besides, we are up to here with other projects to do."

"I know, but this is for such a good cause. I'm sure we can find something special to make. If we do everything Mom said with the stove, I think it will turn out fine."

Elma drew in a quick breath and released it slowly. She'd always had a hard time saying no to her sister. "Oh, all right. I'll do the cooking show with you."

Thelma clapped her hands. "Great! Why don't we try making Grandma's Christmas cake? In fact, since it's so early and we don't have to open the store for a few hours, we can make the cake right now."

Elma pushed away from the table. "If you insist, but let's get some breakfast first, because I'm *hungerich*."

"I'm hungry too." Thelma opened the refrigerator door. "We still have plenty of eggs. Do you want them fried, boiled, scrambled, or poached?"

"Why don't you boil them this time?" Elma suggested. "If you do several, we can have them for a midday snack or sliced on a salad."

"That's what I'll do then." Thelma took out a carton of eggs. "Do you want to get out the ingredients for the cake, while I put the eggs on to boil?"

"Sure." Elma left her seat and took out Grandma's cookbook to look for the recipe. Then she went to the cupboard and gathered all the ingredients. "I'm glad we bought some Jell-O last week when we went shopping, or we wouldn't be able to make this cake."

"That's true. The red and green Jell-O ingredients are what make the cake taste moist and look so colorful and appealing." Thelma grinned. "I'll bet this cake will bring a fairly good price when the bidding starts. I mean, who wouldn't want a delicious festive cake such as this to get them in the mood for Christmas?"

"It's hard to think about Christmas when we have so many other things to do," Elma said, placing a measuring cup on the counter. "I know some of the stores start decorating for the holiday as early as October, but it's not until after Thanksgiving that we even start making out Christmas cards. And we never do any holiday baking until a week before Christmas."

"That's true, but this is different, and our cake will be different, because I'm sure it'll be something that no one else will have at the cooking show to auction off."

Elma shrugged. "I hope you're right about that."

Thelma had put the cake in the oven when she heard the rumble of a vehicle coming up the driveway. "Someone's here," she called to Elma, who had gone to the living room to gather up some throw rugs. Since they'd been letting Tiger in every night, Elma shook the rugs every morning as soon as they put the cat outside, saying that he'd left cat hair behind.

When her sister made no response, Thelma closed the oven door and went to the kitchen window to look out. A delivery truck was coming up the driveway, and when it passed the house, she realized it must be heading for the store.

Cupping her hands around her mouth, she hollered a little louder. "It's a delivery truck, Elma—probably bringing some of the things we ordered for the store. I'm going out there to open the store and tell the driver where to set the boxes. Could you check on the cake while I'm gone?"

Elma mumbled something, so Thelma figured she

must have understood what she'd said. Grabbing a sweater from the back of her kitchen chair, Thelma dashed out the back door. She'd only made it as far as the barn when she realized that her half-slip was sliding down her legs. "Oh my!" Quickly, she opened the barn door and stepped inside. "Now wouldn't that have been embarrassing if my slip had done that when I got to the store? Or I could have tripped on it coming across the yard." She pulled the slip back in place. Thelma couldn't figure out why that had happened. She'd never had one of her slips fall off before. *Maybe I've lost some weight since moving here. I'd better try to eat a little more, and for sure, I'll need to take in the waistband on my slip so that doesn't happen again.*

Continuing on to the store, walking a little slower this time, Thelma made sure to keep her hands pressed firmly against her waist. When she got back to the house, she'd either look for a slip that fit better or pin this one so it was a bit tighter.

When Thelma got to the store, the delivery truck was parked near the basement door. She waved to the driver and shouted, "I'll unlock the door and let you in."

"No problem," the young English man hollered back.

After Thelma unlocked the door, she told him to bring the boxes inside. "You can stack them over there." She motioned to a corner of the basement where some empty cardboard boxes sat.

While the delivery man brought in the boxes, Thelma stood off to one side so she wouldn't be in his way. Since she wasn't walking, she felt certain that her slip would stay in place.

"Do you have a restroom I can use?" the man asked. "I drank too much coffee this morning."

Thelma motioned to the steps leading to the main part of the store. "There's a bathroom upstairs."

"Okay, thanks." He started for the stairs but paused. "Oh, there's one more box on my truck. I'll get it as soon as I'm done in the restroom."

"That's okay," Thelma was quick to say. "I'll go out and get it."

"Are you sure? I mean—"

"It's no problem at all."

When the man went upstairs, Thelma headed outside and climbed into the back of his truck. It didn't take her long to spot the box that was theirs because it was clearly marked. The only problem was she would have to move two boxes that were on top of it. That should be easy enough.

Boy was I ever wrong. Thelma grunted as she struggled to pick up the box on top. *What in the world could be in here that's making it so heavy?*

When Elma stepped onto the back porch to shake the last rug, she spotted a delivery truck parked near the basement entrance of the store. *I'd better go let him in.* "Thelma," she hollered, sticking her head through the open door, "I'm going out to the store to let the driver in."

Hoping her sister had heard, Elma sprinted across the yard and up the path that led to the store. When she got there, she was surprised to see the door open. *Now that's strange. I wonder if we left it open last night.*

Stepping inside, she almost collided with a tall English man. "Oops, sorry," he said. "I didn't realize you'd come back already."

Elma tipped her head. *Come back from where? Does he mean come back from the house?* Before she could voice her thoughts, however, he handed her the shipping invoice and headed out the door. "I think that's everything. See you next time."

As he was getting in the truck, Elma glanced out the open door and gasped. There sat Thelma in the back of his truck, holding a box in her lap.

"Wait up!" Elma shouted, running out the door as the truck started pulling away. "My sister's in the back of your truck!"

The truck kept moving, and Elma chased after it, waving and hollering for the driver to stop. He was about to pull out on the main road, when the truck came to a halt. The young man rolled down his window. "What's going on? Did I forget one of your packages?"

"Not a package." Elma pointed to the back of his truck. "My sister—she's inside your truck." The young man hopped out and ran to the back. He looked at Thelma, whose face was red as a ripe cherry, then he looked back at Elma. "There are two of you?"

Elma nodded. "We're twins."

His brows furrowed as he turned back to Thelma. "What are you doing in my truck?"

"I told you I'd get the last package while you used the restroom, remember?"

He scratched the side of his head. "Oh, yeah, that's right. When I came out of the restroom and saw the person I thought was you in the store, I figured you'd brought the package in."

"It's right here." Thelma handed Elma the box. "It was under two other packages, but they were heavy, so I had a hard time getting it at first."

"Don't ever do that again," he muttered. "From now on, I'll take care of getting all the packages out of the truck. It's actually company policy not to let anyone but the driver in the truck. If your sister hadn't hollered for me to stop, you may have ended up in Michigan before the day was out, and then I would have been in a heap of trouble."

"Sorry about that." Wearing a sheepish expression, Thelma stepped down from the truck, holding the sides of her dress. She headed back to the house, while Elma took the box into the store.

When Thelma opened the door to the house, she was greeted by a haze of smoke. "What's going on?" It didn't take her long to realize the smoke was coming from the kitchen.

Coughing, while covering her nose with her hands, she raced into the room. Seeing smoke billowing from the stove, she jerked the oven door open. "Oh no!" The cake in the pans looked like two blobs of charcoal.

Thelma grabbed two pot holders and removed the pans then carried them out to the porch. After resting them on the pot holders on the porch floor, she raced back inside and opened all the downstairs windows. When she went back outside, Elma was walking toward the house.

"What happened?" Elma asked, pointing to the cake pans.

"The cake is ruined. The layers were left in the oven too long. Didn't you check on them like I asked you?"

Elma's brows furrowed. "When was that?"

"Before I went out to the store to let the delivery man in." Thelma folded her arms. "I told you I was going and asked you to check on the cake."

Elma groaned. "I was singing while gathering the rugs. Guess I didn't hear you. Then when I took the rugs outside to shake them and realized a delivery truck was waiting at the store, I hollered at you so you'd know I was going. I assumed you'd be checking on the cake and taking it out of the oven when it was done."

"Well, I guess you didn't hear me, and I certainly didn't hear you, because I was already at the store."

Elma sank into one of the wicker chairs on the porch. "If we try to make that cake again, I fear something else may happen. Participating in the cooking show is not a good idea, Sister. Is there any way we can get out of it?"

Thelma shook her head determinedly. "And let the community down? No way! We're gonna make that cake, and it will turn out fine."

Chapter 15

"I really wish we weren't obligated to do that cooking show tomorrow," Elma said as her sister took out the ingredients for Grandma's Christmas cake. "We had a busy day at the store, and I'm so tired I can barely keep my eyes open, let alone stay awake long enough to bake a cake."

"Why don't you go up to bed, while I bake the cake?" Thelma suggested.

Elma yawned. "Are you sure about that? I wouldn't feel right about leaving you down here by yourself with that old thing." She gestured to the woodstove. "Remember what happened the last time we used the oven to do a trial run on this cake. Plus, the kitchen took awhile to air out from that burnt smell. If that happens again, we sure couldn't take a coal-black cake to the cooking show to be auctioned."

"I'll be fine," Thelma said. "I know better than to leave the room while the cake is baking. I'll sit out here in the kitchen and get some knitting done till the cake is ready to come out of the oven."

Still feeling a bit hesitant, Elma smiled and said, "Okay. Danki, Sister."

Thelma gave Elma a hug. "Sleep well, and I'll see you in the morning. We have a big day ahead of us, but I'm sure it'll be fun and rewarding."

Elma wasn't sure about the fun part, but she knew that a charity event such as this was important. She hoped she wasn't doing the wrong thing by going to bed early and leaving Thelma to bake the cake by herself.

Thelma was excited about making Grandma's Christmas cake. In addition to the cake itself, two flavors of Jell-O would be used for the filling, with whipped topping and cream cheese for the frosting.

Humming to herself, she followed the directions in Grandma's recipe book then greased the bottom of two nine-inch round pans. "This will be a piece of cake," she murmured, grinning at her pun.

The directions said to bake the cake at 350 degrees for thirty to thirty-five minutes or until done. For the woodstove, that meant she didn't want the oven to get too hot. Placing the cake pans carefully into the oven, Thelma closed the door, set the wind-up timer, and took a seat at the table with a cup of tea and her knitting project. When her folks were visiting, she'd kept her knitting needles and yarn in her room so Mom wouldn't see the gloves she was making for Christmas.

Sure hope our folks can come here for Christmas, Thelma thought as her needles began clicking. She paused for a sip of tea. *I wonder what it'll be like if Elma and I have to spend the holiday alone?* In all the twins' thirty-two years, they'd never been away from their parents for Christmas. It had been so wonderful having them here. As Thelma sat in the quietness of the kitchen, it felt abnormally empty.

The sweet scent of vanilla tickled Thelma's nose as the cakes continued baking. The aroma made her think of Christmas. She reflected on all the Christmases they'd come here to spend with Grandma and Grandpa. The same cake recipe and this old oven were working together once again.

Thelma's gaze settled on the kitchen cupboards. She was glad Dad had been able to put handles on the ones that had been missing. It not only looked better, but it was easier to open the doors too.

Wondering if Grandma had ever sat here sewing while waiting for something in the oven to finish, Thelma resumed knitting. Pretty soon, the timer went off. Grasping one of the oven mitts she'd set out, Thelma opened the oven door and poked a toothpick into each of the cake pans. It came out clean both times, so she was sure they were done. Best of all, neither looked overly brown. *Whew! That's a relief! I'll bet Grandma would be proud of me, and so would Mom.*

She grabbed the other mitt and removed the hot pans from the oven, placing each on its own cooling rack. Then, before she went back to her knitting, Thelma stood over the cakes and inhaled deeply as the steamy aroma rose from both pans. The whole kitchen smelled like Grandma's Christmas cake. Thelma figured any minute now, Elma would appear, since the cake's inviting smell seemed to be wafting through the house.

Thelma tilted her head, waiting to hear footsteps coming down the stairs. No sign of Elma though. *She must be in a sound sleep.*

Half an hour later, Thelma checked the cake pans. They were still slightly warm, but she figured it would be okay to add the Jell-O now. After poking several holes in the first one, she mixed the red Jell-O and carefully spooned the crimson liquid over the top. Then she did the same with the other cake, spooning the warm green Jell-O over that half. When that was done, she covered both cakes with plastic wrap and set them in the refrigerator to cool more thoroughly. The recipe said the cakes should be refrigerated overnight or for a few hours.

I'll probably stay up and finish the cake tonight she told herself. *Otherwise there will be too much to do in the morning.*

Thelma left the kitchen and let Tiger in for the night. She wasn't surprised to find him sitting by the back door. When she opened it, he meowed loudly then pranced inside as though he owned the place. With his tail in the air, Tiger strutted around the living room, purring, until he finally settled down on one of the throw rugs and fell asleep.

Thelma went back to the kitchen and glanced at the clock. It was nine o'clock, so at eleven she would take the pans from the refrigerator, remove the cake rounds, and put them together with filling between each layer. Once the top and sides of the cake had been frosted, she planned to add some red and green sprinkles to make it look more festive. That's what Grandma had always done when she made her special Christmas cake.

Think I'll go downstairs and see how the kittens are doing, Thelma decided. She grabbed her flashlight and headed down the stairs, careful to close the door behind her. If Tiger should awaken, she didn't want him going to the basement and disturbing Misty and her babies.

When Thelma reached the bottom of the stairs, she turned on the overhead gas lamp and headed toward the back of the basement. The kittens' eyes were open now, and they'd become quite active. Thelma knew it wouldn't be long and they'd be getting out of the box. She would either have to find a taller box for them or put up some kind of a barricade. It wouldn't be good to have them wandering all over the basement and possibly getting stuck behind something. They could get hurt.

Leaning down, she scooped up one of the kittens. It purred as she rubbed its head gently against her chin. "All *bopplin* are cute," she murmured. "Human babies more so than others." Unexpected tears sprang to Thelma's eyes. If she remained single the rest of her life, she would never experience the joy of being a mother. *Lord, help me not to long for something I may never have,* she prayed silently.

The words of Philippians 4:11 came to mind: *"For I have learned, in whatsoever state I am, therewith to be content."*

Feeling somewhat better, Thelma remained with the kittens and their mother awhile longer before going back upstairs. Knowing she needed to wash up after handling the cats, she went to the bathroom, where she removed some loose cat hair from her dress and washed her hands.

When she returned to the kitchen, she opened the refrigerator to check on the cakes. It was ten thirty, and she was beginning to feel tired, so she decided to take the cakes out of their pans, since they seemed to have cooled sufficiently. Using a spatula to loosen the cakes, she slid the first one onto a plate. After mixing the whipped topping with the creamed cheese, as per the directions in Grandma's cookbook, she spread some of the creamy white mixture on the first cake round. Then she took out the second cake round and placed it on top of the first.

"Ach!" Thelma gasped. "The top of the cake looks a bit lopsided. I'll need to do something about that."

She pursed her lips. Maybe it wouldn't be too difficult. All she needed to do was add more frosting to the side that looked uneven. "Easy as pie. . . I mean cake." Thelma chuckled as she piled more frosting on the cake and spread it over the area that needed it the most. "Not too bad. I think it looks fine. I'll add a bit more and then do the sides."

Thelma had only added a little frosting to the sides, when Tiger darted into the room and leaped onto the counter, knocking over the bowl. Before Thelma could grab him, the cat swished his paw through the frosting. The next thing she knew, the bowl had rolled off the counter and landed upside down on the floor.

"Oh no! Get down, you bad cat!" Thelma groaned as Tiger leaped onto the floor and licked the frosting smeared on his paws. "I can't use that topping now." She didn't have another tub of whipped cream, and no creamed cheese either, so there was no way she could make another batch of icing. About all Thelma could do at this point was to add some sprinkles on the top, which she did right away. Once that was done, the cake looked a little better, though not the way she remembered Grandma's Christmas cake, which had always looked perfect.

"It'll have to do." Thelma put the cake inside a plastic container and attached the lid. When she went to place it in the refrigerator she realized that the receptacle was too big. Placing it back on the counter, Thelma rearranged some of the items in the refrigerator. Then she picked up the container and tried once more. This time it fit, but with only an inch to spare.

She and Elma would only have to demonstrate how to bake the cake tomorrow then show this cake to the audience so they could see the finished product. She would simply explain that it was lacking some of the frosting.

Of course, she thought as she turned off the gas lamp, *I still haven't told Elma that we'll be expected to stand up in front of everyone and do all the prep work for the cake. If she knew that, she'd probably refuse to go.*

Chapter 16

When Elma entered the kitchen the next morning, she found her sister fixing a pot of tea. *"Guder mariye."*

"Good morning." Thelma smiled. "You look rested. Did you sleep well last night?"

"Jah, I did. How about you?"

"Not as soundly as I would have liked, but it's my fault for getting to bed late."

"How come you stayed up?" Elma questioned.

"I was frosting the cake." Thelma grabbed a couple of floral-patterned cups from the cupboard and set them by the plates on the table. "The icing I sampled was quite tasty. Even the cat had a taste of it."

"I'm glad the frosting was good, but how'd the cake turn out?" Elma sniffed the delicious aroma of peppermint tea. "It didn't get too done, I hope."

Thelma shook her head. "When the cake was finished it was a warm golden brown." She motioned to the boiled eggs on the table. "I think we'd better eat so we can get ready to go to Shipshe. We don't want to be late this morning."

Elma sighed. "About the only good part of going there today is knowing that we'll be taking Pearl and not Rusty."

"Actually, we won't be taking Pearl after all."

"How come?" Elma's shoulders slumped a bit.

"When I went out to the barn earlier to get her, I

discovered that she'd thrown a shoe."

"That's not good." Elma frowned. "I don't want to take Rusty."

"I know, and I'll call the local farrier as soon as we get home." Thelma gave Elma's arm a light tap. "Don't worry. I'll be in the driver's seat. I'm gonna follow the advice Dad gave me when he was here."

"What advice was that?"

"I'll take control and let Rusty know that he has to obey my commands."

"I hope it works, because I'm not in the mood for his antics this morning." Though Elma wasn't happy about taking Rusty, at least the responsibility of getting him there was not hers. She hoped he would behave himself this time.

The twins were halfway to Shipshewana when Rusty started lunging and lurching.

"What is that horse's problem?" Elma touched her sister's arm.

"I have no idea, but he'd better settle down." Thelma's jaw clenched so hard, Elma could hear her teeth snap together.

Elma's back hurt as she sat firmly on the seat. "Maybe we should turn around and go home."

With a determined expression, Thelma shook her head. "I'm sure he'll settle down. Hold on to your seat so you don't get jostled." Her stern, take-control voice kicked in, and Thelma handled Rusty in a manner a lot like Dad would have used.

Elma did as her sister suggested, the whole time praying they would get to their destination safely. Finally— and much to Elma's relief—the horse settled down. When they pulled up to the hitching rail near the Shipshewana Event Center, Elma climbed out of the buggy and secured Rusty.

"I'll get the cake from the back," Thelma said after

she'd stepped down from her seat. "Oh, and Sister, before we go in, there's something I need to tell you."

"What's that?" Elma asked.

"When our names are called and we have to take our cake onstage before the bidding starts, we'll need to demonstrate how to make the cake first."

Elma stiffened and her mouth went dry. "Are you saying we have to make the cake in front of all those people?"

Thelma gave a quick nod.

"But we don't have the necessary ingredients for that. All we brought was the finished cake, which, by the way, I haven't seen yet."

Thelma patted Elma's arm. "You'll see it when I take it out of the container, but that won't happen till we've finished our demonstration."

"Which we can't do without the ingredients," Elma reminded.

"I brought them along." Thelma motioned to the back of the buggy. "They're in that cardboard box with the cake. When I went to the grocery store in Topeka the other day, I got enough flour, milk, and other ingredients we need for the cake." She smiled. "I even brought a large bowl, wooden spoon, and a wire whisk along."

"What about the whipped topping and cream cheese to frost the cake?"

"We won't have to worry about that part. All we have to show the audience is how to mix the cake, put it into the pans, and place it in the oven. Then we'll take our finished cake out of the container and show them that," Thelma explained. "Now would you like to carry the box, or should I?"

"I'll do it," Elma mumbled. It all sounded simple enough, but a sense of panic set in. The thought of cooking in front of a group of people, many of whom they would not know, made Elma nervous. She wondered if they'd made a big mistake coming here today.

"Let's take a seat in the front row so we can see everything and be close to the stage," Thelma suggested when they entered the building. Already, hundreds of people were milling around.

"I wish we could sit in the back and watch the proceedings." Elma's voice trembled a bit. "Look at all these people. I had no idea this event would draw such a big crowd."

"If we sit in the back, we'll have farther to walk when our names are called." Thelma tugged on her sister's arm. "Let's look for a good seat before they're all gone."

When the twins found chairs in the first row, Elma set the box on the floor by her feet.

Looking at the stage in front of them, Thelma saw a stove with an oven, a long table, and several plastic bins full of cooking supplies, as well as a large pitcher of water.

The room was astir with people chatting and others still straggling in, looking for a place to sit or stand. Finally, things settled down as a tall English woman took the stage and turned on a microphone. Elma leaned close to Thelma and whispered, "We won't have to say anything while we're mixing the ingredients for the cake, I hope."

All Thelma could do was shrug, for the woman in charge had begun speaking. "Welcome to our cooking show charity event," she said. "We appreciate all of you who came out today. This event is something special for our community, since the money is going to a good cause. Because of that, we hope you will be generous with your bids and enjoy the show."

Everyone clapped. Once the applause died down, the woman continued. "Thank you for such a warm welcome. To begin our program, we have two single ladies from Topeka. Elma and Thelma Hochstetler, would you please come up?"

"Here we go." Elma picked up the box, and Thelma followed onto the stage. "I didn't know we'd be the first ones," Elma whispered.

Thelma put on her best smile. "Don't worry. Afterward we can relax and watch everyone else."

Elma's face turned ashen when the host handed her the microphone. "Please tell us a little about your dessert and why you chose to make it today."

Thelma thought she could hear her sister's knees knocking as she said in a quavering voice, "This is our Grandma's Christmas cake. We chose it in memory of her."

The audience clapped, and Thelma noticed pink splotches had erupted on Elma's cheeks. Her own face felt warm too.

After Thelma placed the ingredients on the table, Elma picked up the recipe card. As she read the instructions, Thelma measured the ingredients. *So far, so good.*

Glancing at the audience, Thelma's throat constricted. So many people, and they were all watching her and Elma. She didn't realize being the center of attention would make her this nervous. Averting her gaze, she hurriedly mixed the flour and other dry ingredients. In the process, Thelma ended up with a puff of white on her dress, and some settled on her arm. Brushing it away, she looked at the snickering audience again. All eyes seemed to be focused on them.

"Be careful, Sister," Elma warned. "You're getting flour all over the place. By the way, you need to add the eggs and milk."

"I—I know. I feel like I'm all thumbs right now," Thelma muttered under her breath.

"It's okay. It's okay. Try to stay calm," Elma whispered. But her words were not reassuring.

Thelma frantically grabbed more flour and dumped it into the bowl.

"Sister, you're not making bread."

Thelma snickered. She didn't know what else to do.

Then, in her nervous state, she managed to spill what was left in the bag of flour onto the floor. "Oh no!"

At the same time, the twins leaned down to reach for an egg and bumped heads. When they stood, they rubbed the spots of impact simultaneously. Another round of chuckles came from the crowd, making Thelma even more nervous.

With shaky fingers, she managed to crack the eggs into the bowl, but the shells fell in as well. "Oh my word!" Thelma's cheeks felt like they were on fire as she hastily picked out the pieces. This was not going well. She could only imagine what people must be thinking. *They probably think we're a couple of bumbling* dummkepp *who don't know a thing about baking a cake.*

"Is there anything I can do to help?" the host of the show asked.

As Thelma shook her head, Elma rolled her eyes.

"Pour the milk," Elma said impatiently, nudging Thelma's arm.

"I will. Don't rush me." Thelma picked up the carton of milk, but her hands shook so badly, she ended up pouring all of it into the bowl.

"Oh no, that's too much." Elma handed Thelma the microphone and grabbed the wire whisk. "Let me take over now."

"I don't see how you're gonna fix that mess, Sister," Thelma said, her mouth too close to the mic. Her eyes widened, and the audience roared.

When Elma stirred the batter, a glob splattered up and stuck to the end of her nose.

Thelma's chuckle resonated through the microphone, as she pointed at Elma. Despite their best efforts, this was turning into an unrehearsed skit.

"I know that young woman—or at least one of them," Delbert said, bumping Joseph with his elbow.

Joseph's forehead wrinkled. "I know one of 'em too.

Well, maybe not *know*, but I did meet her at the hardware store in Topeka a few weeks ago."

"I met one of the twins at the hardware store here in Shipshe." Delbert rubbed his chin. "Didn't realize there were two of them though. Thought I was seein' one woman in two places."

"They must be identical, because they sure look alike." Joseph leaned forward in his chair. "I'm tryin' to figure out which one of 'em I saw in Topeka."

"They're sure funny." Delbert chuckled when the twin wearing the green dress stuck her hand in the bowl to fish out the spoon her sister had dropped. "I wonder if they're really that clumsy or just puttin' on an act to get the spectators enthused so they'll make a high bid on their cake."

"I don't know." Joseph leaned close to Delbert's ear. "I really want that cake."

Delbert looked at Joseph as though he had two heads. "You haven't even seen it yet."

"I know, but I want to meet that young woman."

"Which one?"

"The one who's holding the microphone now. Don't know why, but the more I watch her, the more I'm thinkin' she's the woman I met in Topeka."

"Oh boy." Delbert grunted. "What are we dealin' with here—love at first sight?"

Joseph shook his head. "I'd like the chance to get to know her, and that won't happen unless I get the cake." The determined set of his friend's jaw told Delbert that Joseph was serious about this.

"After the cooking show's over, go on up and talk to her, Joe."

Joseph slunk down in his chair. "I can't do that, Dell. She'd think I was too bold. But if I bid on her cake and win, I'll have a reason to speak with her when I get the cake."

Delbert shrugged. "Suit yourself. If you want the cake, go ahead and bid. But if I were you, I'd at least wait till they show the audience what the finished cake looks like. You might not even want it."

"But if I do, would you bid on it for me?"

Delbert's eyebrows rose. "Why would I bid on it? You're the one who wants it."

"I—I know, but if I try to call out a bid, I'll get tongue-tied and start stuttering."

"Here's what I've got to say about that. If you really want to meet the girl, then you'll call out the bid, even if you have to trip over your own tongue."

Joseph kept his gaze straight ahead. He'd wait until he saw the finished cake and then try to persuade his friend to do the bidding. After all, Dell had told him several times that he'd do almost anything for him.

Chapter 17

The cake pans were finally in the oven, and it was time for Thelma to remove the cake they had brought from its container. Placing it on the table, she faced the audience, removed the lid, and lifted the cake plate out. "Oh no," she murmured, staring in disbelief. Their cake was even more lopsided than it had been last night. The trip to Shipshewana, with Rusty acting up, had obviously not helped.

Thelma looked at Elma, who was clearly upset. "What happened to our cake?" Elma whispered, giving her a sidelong glance. "It looks *baremlich*."

Thelma couldn't argue with that; the cake did look terrible. Not only was the top lopsided, but the frosting barely covered the sides. What icing was left on the cake seemed to have accumulated on the plate, around the base. The cake must not have been cool enough, which had caused the frosting to run. *No one will ever bid on this now. We ought to leave the stage,* Thelma thought. *I'll explain things later,* she mouthed to Elma.

A middle-aged English man approached the stage with some paperwork. He talked to the woman in charge, and when they parted, he grabbed the microphone.

"All right now, who'll start the bidding with five dollars?" he shouted.

Thelma gulped, feeling trapped by the audience. There was no way they could leave the stage—at least not until they'd become thoroughly embarrassed, because she was certain no one would place even one bid on this pitiful cake. *I should have listened to my sister and gotten out of this event.*

Joseph leaned over and whispered something.

"What was that, Joe?" Delbert asked.

Joseph's ears turned pink, like they always did when he was embarrassed. "I need you to bid on the cake for me."

Delbert frowned. "Why would you want a lopsided cake?"

"It's for a good cause, and I want to meet that girl. Come on, Dell. I'll give you the money for it."

"Okay, but you're gonna owe me for this." Delbert lifted his hand. "Five dollars!"

"I'll make it ten!"

Delbert looked at Joseph, and they both looked around the room. Where had that deep voice come from, upping the bid?

"Fifteen," Joseph whispered. "Hurry, Dell, do it now."

"Fifteen dollars!" Delbert shouted. Looking at Joseph, he chuckled. "Think I'm getting into this bidding game, especially since I'm spending your money."

"Twenty!" the other bidder hollered.

Delbert looked at his buddy again, and when Joseph nodded, Delbert raised his hand and upped the bid—this time for thirty dollars.

Excitement wafted over the crowd. Some people even clapped.

"Fifty dollars!" the other man shouted, a little louder this time. Was there no stopping this fellow? Why was he so desperate to have a pathetic-looking cake?

"Go higher," Joseph prompted, bumping Delbert's arm. "Take it up to sixty."

Delbert raised his hand again. "Sixty dollars!"

"Seventy!"

Joseph, rocking back and forth in his chair, looked almost desperate. "Go to eighty. I—I want that c–cake." He wiped his sweaty forehead. The poor guy had started stuttering. Delbert knew he'd better get that cake, no matter what it cost. He cupped his hands around his mouth and shouted, "Eighty dollars!"

By this time, the audience was in an uproar. Some people stood, and even more applauded. Delbert and Joseph kept their eyes on the auctioneer.

"Eighty dollars once... Eighty dollars twice... Do we have another bid on this unusual cake?"

Delbert watched the two women onstage, holding the cake with quizzical expressions. They were probably as surprised as the audience that two men were bidding on their crazy-looking dessert.

"I'll make it ninety!" the other bidder bellowed.

The crowd whooped and hollered even louder. Several started shouting, "Higher! Higher! Higher!"

Delbert looked at Joseph. "Now what?" He glanced around, trying to see who was bidding against him, but it was so crowded, he couldn't tell.

"Go again, Dell. Make it one hundred." Joseph pointed his finger toward the ceiling. "Raise the bid. Hurry, please."

Delbert's hand shot up. "One hundred dollars!"

"One hundred going once. . . One hundred going twice. . ."

Delbert held his breath, waiting to see if the deep voice would speak again and outbid him, but all was quiet.

"Sold—to the man wearing a blue shirt in the fourth row!"

"Th–that's you," Joseph said a bit too loud, jumping up. "You won the cake!"

The audience clapped again. Those folks closest to Delbert congratulated him. Someone patted his shoulder. Joseph slunk down in his seat. The auctioneer slowly shook his head. Delbert was glad it was over.

Now a part of the audience again, Elma sat next to her sister, watching the rest of the contestants. After each demonstration and bidding was completed, she was surprised to see that, so far, their cake had brought in the most money.

Glancing around the crowd then settling her gaze a few rows back on the Amish man who'd won their cake, Elma quickly turned her attention back to the stage, embarrassed when he caught her staring. "Do you think this show will be over soon?" she whispered to Thelma.

"Aren't you having a good time?"

Elma fidgeted in her chair. "Guess I am, but my stomach is starting to growl, and I can't stop thinking of all the things that need to be done at home."

Thelma patted Elma's hand. "This is the last item up for bid. As soon as it's over, we can give our cake to the man who won it then get a little something to eat before we run a few errands and head for home."

Elma's nerves escalated. If standing onstage in front of all those people hadn't been bad enough, now they'd have to give the lopsided cake to the man who'd bid that outrageous price of one hundred dollars.

When the cooking show let out, Joseph asked Delbert if he would go with him to speak to the twins, because he was too nervous to speak to them alone.

"I suppose I should," Delbert said. "I must admit, once I got into that bidding war, it became an exciting game—especially when the crowd starting urging me on. And after all I went through to get you that cake, I'd like the chance to meet those twins. When the woman in charge first introduced them, she said they were single."

"Which of the women are you interested in?" Joseph hoped it wasn't the same twin he had his eye on. But they looked so much alike, he couldn't be sure which one he'd met in Topeka. *What if I can't talk to her without stuttering?*

Delbert shrugged. "I'm not sure which one I met before. Right now I'm thinking the more serious one."

"Not the twin who was holding the lopsided cake?"

"Nope. Did you see the look of disapproval on her sister's face when she took that dessert out of its container?"

Joseph nodded. "I wonder how it got that way."

"We'll never know if we don't talk to them." Delbert thumped Joseph's back. "I see 'em by the table where all the other baked goods are. Let's head over there now."

When the men approached Thelma and Elma, Joseph couldn't think of a single thing to say. He stared at the twins, feeling rather foolish.

"I'm Delbert Gingerich, and this is my friend, Joseph Beechy," Delbert spoke up. "I'm the one who gave the winning bid, but it was really for him."

Joseph's face felt like it was on fire.

"That was an interesting presentation you ladies gave." Delbert chuckled. "The humor you added really got the audience enthused. Did you plan it that way?"

The twins looked at each other with strange expressions. Then the one wearing the green dress spoke up. "It was definitely not planned. I think I speak for my sister when I say that we were both nervous wrecks."

"That's right," the other twin agreed. "We've never cooked anything in a public setting before. I was surprised that anyone even bid on our crazy-looking cake, much less paid so much for it."

Joseph, finally finding his voice, said, "It didn't l–look like you were n–nervous." *Not like I feel right now,* he mentally added.

"Which one of you is Elma and which one is Thelma?" Delbert asked.

"I'm Elma," the twin wearing the blue dress said. "And this is my sister, Thelma."

Delbert moved closer to the twins. "If I'm not mistaken, I bumped into one of you at Yoder's Hardware about a month ago."

"That was me," Thelma spoke up. "It was when you were waiting at the checkout counter and you dropped your things."

Delbert snickered. "That was pretty clumsy of me."

"I met one of y–you too," Joseph stuttered. "It was—"

"At the hardware store in Topeka." Thelma finished his sentence. "That was me as well."

Elma smiled. "Apparently, you've both met my sister before."

"Where do you live?" Delbert asked.

"Our home is in Topeka," Elma said. "We moved there from Sullivan, Illinois, after our grandparents died. They left us their house and variety store. Where do you men live?"

"We're both from LaGrange," Delbert said before Joseph could find his voice. It seemed like Delbert was taking over the conversation. Joseph sure hoped his friend wasn't interested in Thelma.

They talked awhile longer, and then Delbert suggested that Joseph pick up the cake so they could get going.

"We should probably go too," Thelma said. "We want to grab a bite to eat and then head for home soon after. Our grandparents' house is pretty run-down and in need of repairs. We may paint the living room this afternoon."

Delbert reached into his pocket and pulled out a business card. "I'm a carpenter with my own woodworking business. If you need any repairs done that involve carpentry, please consider giving me a call."

Elma smiled. "You may be hearing from us."

As the men turned away, Joseph nudged Delbert's arm. "If they call you to go look at their place, I'd like to go along." He walked with a spring in his step.

Delbert grinned and thumped Joseph's shoulder. "Sure, no problem."

As Thelma and Elma headed for home after a quick bite to eat, they talked and even laughed about their lopsided cake. "At first I was mortified," Elma said. "But everything turned out pretty well in the end. I feel good knowing that our contribution went to a good cause."

"Jah." Thelma held firmly to Rusty's reins. "In addition to our cake going for such a high bid, we got to meet two very nice fellows." She glanced over at Elma. "Do you think we should call Delbert and see how much he would charge to fix our sagging front porch?"

Elma nodded. "Since Dad gave us that money, maybe we can afford to hire Delbert to do the work. In addition to making our place look nicer, it'll be a lot safer."

"You're right," Thelma agreed. "Honestly, I fear that someone will step right through the old wood and get hurt."

Elma sat up straight and loosened her sweater. "Whew! It's sure getting warm in this buggy."

I wish it were Joseph we'd be calling to work on our house, Thelma thought. *But I'd better accept the fact that I might never see him again.*

Chapter 18

The following Saturday, when Elma came into the house after checking messages in the phone shack, she smiled at Thelma and said, "Remember when I left a message for Delbert Gingerich the other day?"

Thelma placed a clean dish in the drying rack. "Jah. Did you hear something back from him?"

"I did. His message said that he would be out later today."

Thelma smiled, putting a freshly washed glass on the rack. "That's good to hear. I hope he's willing to fix our porch and that it won't cost too much. It would be nice if we didn't have to use all the money Dad gave us on just one project." She rinsed some pieces of silverware and set them in the dish drainer to dry.

"I agree. If Delbert's able to do it and we have some money left over, maybe we can ask him to do a few other projects."

Thelma grabbed a clean dish towel and began drying the dishes. "That would be good."

"It will be nice to see him again. He seemed like a pleasant man." Elma grabbed her to-do list and took a seat at the table. "What do you think would be the second thing we could ask him to do?"

Thelma finished drying a glass and put in the cupboard. "How about putting on some nice cabinet doors beneath this old sink? That would look better than the outdated curtain."

"You're right, Sister. That would be a good thing to have done." Elma jotted it down.

"So it's Delbert you're interested in, and not his friend Joseph?"

Elma tapped her pencil against her chin. "What makes you think I'm interested in Delbert?"

"You said it would be nice to see him again, and—"

"Now don't get any silly ideas," Elma interrupted. "He will be coming here to work, not for courting."

Thelma set her dish towel aside and sat across from Elma. "If he showed an interest in you, what would you do?"

Elma blinked her eyes rapidly. "I really can't say, since that hasn't happened."

"But if it did?" Thelma persisted.

"I give up!" Elma lifted her hands in the air. "I can tell that you're not going to drop this subject till I come up with an answer."

"That's right."

"If Delbert were to show some interest in me, I may be interested too. But I'd have to get to know him first to see how well we're suited." Elma leaned closer to Thelma. "Is that the answer you were looking for?"

Thelma grinned, bobbing her head. "Of course, it would be more fun if we both had suitors. Think of all the things we could do as courting couples."

"Maybe Delbert could fix you up with his friend Joseph. You did mention the other day that you thought he was *gutguckich*." Elma tugged the tie on her headscarf.

"I didn't say he was handsome. I said he was cute. Delbert's the handsome one, with that shiny blond hair."

"You're right about that." Elma placed her pencil on the table. "We can't sit here all day and talk about something that may never happen. We need to get out to the store before any customers show up."

"Okay, but I'm going to check on the horses first. I want to make sure that Pearl is happy in her new home."

"Speaking of Pearl," Elma said, as Thelma started for

the door, "since she got new shoes put on last Monday, we can use her instead of Rusty when we need to go somewhere."

Thelma shook her head. "If he's not worked with, he'll never become fully road trained. You can take Pearl whenever you need to go somewhere with the buggy, but I'll keep using Rusty." Her face brightened. "I haven't given up hope on him yet, and I'm going to hang in there till I produce a wonderful buggy horse. Besides, I'm getting more confident each time I take him out."

"That's your choice," Elma said, "but you need to be careful, because you never know what that animal might do."

"I know, and I will be careful." Thelma smiled and scooted out the door.

The twins had closed the store for the day, when Delbert showed up. Thelma was surprised and pleased to see that Joseph was with him.

Looking shyly at Thelma, Joseph mumbled, "I—I came along 'cause Delbert owes me a meal."

"That's right," Delbert agreed. "We're planning to eat at Tiffany's here in Topeka."

"We've never eaten there," Thelma said, "but we hear they have good food."

"If you have no other plans, maybe you'd like to join us for supper," Delbert suggested.

Elma was about to say that she planned to fix a meat loaf, but Thelma spoke first. "We'd be happy to go to Tiffany's, wouldn't we, Sister?"

Feeling like a bug trapped in a spider's web, all Elma could do was nod. It wasn't that she didn't want to go to supper with these men. She simply felt like things were moving too fast. After all, they'd only met Joseph and Delbert last week, and here the men were asking them to share a meal at a restaurant. Maybe Delbert was only being polite. It could be that after Joseph said they were going out to eat, Delbert felt obligated to invite the twins to join them. But there was no point in mulling this over; she and Thelma had already agreed to go.

"Maybe I should take a look at your porch," Delbert suggested.

"That's a good idea," Thelma spoke up. "Let's head over there now."

When they stepped onto the porch, Delbert released a low whistle. "This is sagging pretty badly." He kicked at a couple of boards with the toe of his boot. "I'd say several pieces of this wood are rotted."

Elma cringed. "Does that mean it's going to be expensive to fix?"

"Not necessarily," he replied. "It's gonna depend on what I find when I start tearing into it. I can give you an estimate, but it might go over that amount. I'll try to work within your budget though."

Thelma smiled. "We appreciate that. Don't we, Sister?"

"Of course." Elma wondered if they should have gotten another carpenter to look at the porch too, but if Delbert did the job, it would give her a chance to get to know him better. She could tell from the rosy color on her sister's cheeks that she was glad Joseph had come along with Delbert today too.

When they entered Tiffany's, Joseph made sure he was sitting across the table from Thelma, which put Delbert across from Elma. Earlier at the twins' house, he wasn't sure which twin was who, because they looked so much alike. But after listening to them, he quickly realized that Thelma was more talkative and had a sense of humor.

Despite Joseph's shyness, on the buggy ride over, he'd managed to carry on a conversation with Thelma but mostly because she had so much to say. He wondered, now that they were at the restaurant, if she would continue to carry the conversation, or was she all talked out?

"How did the painting go last week, when you went home after the show?" Joseph managed to ask.

"It went pretty well," Thelma replied. "We got all the furniture moved to the middle of the room, and with two of us painting, we had the walls done in a few hours. The color looks nice too—like the shade of wheat."

When their waitress, a middle-aged Amish woman, came to take their order, everyone agreed that they would have the all-you-can-eat buffet. "Oh, and could you please bring some extra napkins?" Thelma asked.

"No problem. I'll grab you some and bring out your waters." She stuffed her pencil in her apron pocket and headed off toward the kitchen.

"Should we pray now, before we go to the buffet?" Delbert asked.

Joseph bobbed his head. "That's a good idea."

All heads bowed, and when Joseph opened his eyes, their waitress returned with glasses of water. She also handed Thelma a whole stack of napkins.

Thelma snickered. "I wonder why she gave me so many. Maybe I look like a messy person."

"I'm sure she was only being helpful." Elma patted her sister's hand. "And I doubt she thought they were just for you."

Thelma handed each of them three napkins and laid the rest beside her plate. Then they made their way to the buffet.

When they returned to the table with their plates full of fried chicken, mashed potatoes, roast beef, corn, and noodles, Joseph was more than ready to eat. Just smelling the delicious food made his mouth water.

"Too bad they're out of the butterfly shrimp," Delbert commented. "I was kinda hoping for that. Truth is, I like all kinds of seafood."

"Same here," Thelma agreed. "And I like freshwater fish too."

"Do you ever go fishing?" Joseph asked, and he didn't even stutter.

She nodded enthusiastically. "Ever since I was a little

girl and my daed took me out to the lake near our home, I've been hooked on fishing." She covered her mouth and giggled.

Joseph laughed too. He enjoyed Thelma's humor. She was bubbly, and the more he was with her, the more relaxed he became. Not only that, but she was a fine-looking woman. *I wonder how old she and her sister are? Do I dare ask?* Deciding that it would be too bold, he said instead, "If you and Elma aren't busy, maybe you'd like to go fishing with me and Delbert. We're planning to go next Saturday. Would that be a good day for you?"

"Oh, we'd love to go!" Thelma's face broke into a wide smile. "Wouldn't we, Sister?"

Elma, looking none too enthused, slowly nodded. "I—I suppose we could do that, but we'd have to close the store that day."

"That shouldn't be a problem," Thelma said, before taking a drink of water. "We closed it to go to the cooking show, and since it'll be open for business Monday through Friday, I think we deserve a little break, don't you?"

Again Elma nodded, but Joseph sensed she'd rather not go. *Maybe I shouldn't have said anything, but I'd like the chance to get to know Thelma better. Since we all like to fish, it should be a fun day.* He glanced at Delbert and realized that his friend hadn't made a single comment about taking the twins fishing. *I wonder if he'd prefer that they not go. Or maybe he's too busy eating his fried chicken to join the conversation right now.*

Joseph was having such a good time that he really didn't care what Delbert thought. Besides, the fishing trip would give Delbert a chance to get to know Elma better too.

At home after the men dropped the twins off, Thelma brought up the topic of Joseph and Delbert. "You were kind of quiet during supper," she said, sipping her cup of chamomile tea while holding a peanut butter cookie.

"Weren't you having a good time?"

"It was fine. I enjoyed the meal." Elma blew on her tea. "I only wish you hadn't told Joseph that we'd go fishing with them." She sighed, finally taking her first cookie. "You know I don't like to fish. I don't have the patience for it."

"Don't worry about fishing. You can bring a book along. Anyway, it'll be a chance for us to get to know Delbert and Joseph better." Thelma smiled. "I think Joe likes me, Sister. And I have a hunch that Delbert may be a good match for you."

Finished with her snack, Elma said, "I'll admit, I am attracted to his good looks, but I don't know yet whether he and I are compatible."

"Which is why we need to go fishing with them. It'll be a relaxing, fun day—the perfect opportunity to visit and get to know what they're like."

"I suppose."

Thelma placed her hand over Elma's and gave it a gentle squeeze. "You know, this could be our one hope of finding husbands."

Elma finished drinking her tea. "We'll have to wait and see about that."

Chapter 19

"How come you're bringing all of that?" Thelma asked when she noticed Elma stuffing several items into two large tote bags she'd placed on the kitchen table.

Elma blinked, as though surprised at Thelma's question. "We might need all these things. Remember, Mom would say that you never know what can occur on any outing, and being prepared is always good." Elma stood by her totes with her arms folded. "Did you remember to check on all the animals this morning?"

"Jah, I did. They are fed and content, and so are the mama cat and her babies in the basement."

"What about the eggs? Did you collect them like usual?"

Thelma nodded with a sigh. "I did all of that. And why do you always have to remind me of everything?"

"Because you're often preoccupied—this morning, more than usual."

Thelma lifted her gaze to the ceiling. In addition to a first-aid kit, her sister had packed bug spray, disinfectant wipes, blankets, sunglasses, and two umbrellas. "I'm glad we were able to get our fishing licenses earlier this week, and I'm looking forward to meeting Joseph and Delbert at the pond they told us about. If they were picking us up and we went in one buggy, there might not be room for all those things." Thelma glanced at the totes again.

Elma simply went to the refrigerator and took out the sandwiches she'd made to share with the men for lunch.

Along with those, the twins were bringing potato chips, pretzels, cut-up veggies, and grapes. For dessert, they'd baked chocolate chip cookies. Delbert had volunteered to bring beverages, and Joseph would provide the fishing bait.

Thelma had been looking forward to this day ever since they'd made plans with the guys a week ago. Even though she'd only met Joseph, she found him to be quite pleasant. He seemed a bit shy and, except for small talk, hadn't said a lot during their meal at Tiffany's. Maybe that was because she had monopolized too much of the conversation. Joseph was a good listener though. He seemed interested in everything she'd said. It was a good thing she and Elma had chosen to wear different-colored dresses today. That would help the guys to keep them straight. Thelma had double-checked the way she looked this morning, as she wanted to make a nice impression on Joseph. She was even debating about going back to the bathroom and checking one more time to make sure her head covering was on straight.

"I am not really that interested in fishing." Elma broke into Thelma's thoughts.

"Then why'd you agree to go?"

"I did it for you—because I know you like to fish." Elma paused and put a package of paper plates in the wicker basket, along with the chips and cookies. The sandwiches would go in their small cooler. "And I can tell you're smitten with Joseph."

Thelma tipped her head. "Aren't you interested in Delbert? Have you forgotten so soon how handsome he is?"

"You're right, but good looks are not that important." Elma smiled. "I would like the chance to get to know him better though."

"Then it's settled. I have a feeling that by the end of the day, we'll both know more about those men."

LaGrange

"This will be a great day for fishing, and the weather is looking favorable. The sun is shining, and I'm feelin' the warmth," Joseph said as he climbed into Delbert's buggy, which looked sharp and clean, as usual. Recently, Delbert had installed a new heater in the dash of his buggy, but they wouldn't need that today. If Joseph didn't know better, he'd think it was late summer, instead of the middle of October.

Truth was, all week Joseph had been looking forward to this day and getting an opportunity to spend it with Thelma. While he didn't know much about her yet, she'd said she liked to fish. He hoped they'd get some time alone to visit and that he'd discover other things they both liked.

Delbert took up the reins. "Let's hope the fish are biting and the women bring something good for lunch."

"I'm sure they will." Joseph smiled. "Thelma said she was going to bake chocolate chip cookies."

"Sure hope they look better than that crazy cake she and her sister made."

"The cake may not have looked so good, but it sure was tasty. You're lucky I shared it with you."

Delbert guided his horse onto the main road. "You almost had to share it, since I'm the one who got that lopsided dessert for you."

"That's true." Joseph rubbed his chin. "You know, we never did ask the twins how that cake ended up looking so uneven or why the whole thing wasn't frosted."

Delbert thumped Joseph's arm. "Not a problem. You can ask them today."

"You don't think they'll forget about meeting us, do you?"

"Naw. I'm sure they'll remember."

"Can't you make your horse go any faster?" Joseph couldn't help feeling impatient.

"Hold your horses. Snickers is going fast enough." Delbert chuckled. "I want to stop at the store and get some sweet tea."

"What if the twins aren't able to find the pond we told 'em about?" Joseph continued to stroke his chin, trying to keep from becoming too antsy. At least he'd remembered to shave this morning. He'd been so excited about seeing Thelma again he'd almost left the house without doing that. "Maybe we should have gone over to their place to pick them up."

"I gave them good instructions," Delbert said. "Since the small fishing hole is halfway between LaGrange and Topeka, it only made sense that we should meet them there. Now, quit fretting and relax."

As soon as Elma pulled Pearl into the designated spot where Delbert and Joseph had said they would meet, Thelma climbed down and secured the horse to a tree. It was nice that Elma had driven today. She seemed happy to have Pearl pulling their buggy too. *I'm glad I told Dad about Elma's fear of Rusty and he decided to bring our docile, dependable horse.*

"Are you sure this is the right pond?" Elma asked when she joined Thelma by the tree. "I don't see any sign of the men, and no one else seems to be here fishing either." She made a sweeping gesture of the area.

"We followed Delbert's directions, so this has to be the place." Thelma didn't admit it, but she was a little worried too that they might be at the wrong pond.

"Let's leave everything in the buggy till the men arrive. I wouldn't want to have to put it all away if they don't show up." Elma opened the bag of grapes and popped one into her mouth.

"You're right." Thelma walked around for a bit, surveying the pond and enjoying the warmth of the day. It was interesting how the weather could change so quickly. Yesterday it had been chilly with a bit of rain, and now this morning, the sun shone brightly. The sun's warmth felt so good. *How silly of Elma to bring those umbrellas along,* she mused. *I doubt we'll see any rain today.*

Elma swatted at a bothersome fly as she stood stroking Pearl's mane. Even the fly was fooled by the temperatures, but Elma was glad the gnats and most of the other aggravating bugs were gone. *I wonder how long we should wait. If they don't get here soon, maybe we should return home, because I sure don't want to drive my poor horse all over the place in search of the right pond.*

She glanced at Thelma, who stood near the water's edge, looking up at the sky. Elma looked up too. The sky was as blue as ever, without the hint of a cloud. Even so, it might not be like that later in the day, which was the reason she'd come prepared. Her sister may think she was silly bringing all those other things as well, but Elma thought it was good to be prepared for any given situation. Besides, they had plenty of room in their buggy, so what did it hurt?

Tired of waiting, she was about to suggest they go home, when a horse and buggy rolled into the clearing. It was Delbert and Joseph. "Sister, they're here!"

Thelma came running with an eager expression. "Oh good. Now we can begin fishing!"

Elma gritted her teeth. *Oh good. I can't wait.*

"So glad you two were able to find this place," Joseph said, smiling at Thelma. At least he thought it was her. When she spoke, he was sure he would know for certain, but he wished the twins didn't look so much alike. It was confusing.

"It wasn't hard at all, was it, Elma?"

Elma shook her head "We had no problem finding the pond, but when we got here and saw no sign of you and Delbert, we wondered if we were at the wrong place."

"Sorry we're a bit late," Delbert spoke up. "We stopped by the store on the way here so we could pick up some bottles of sweet tea." He gestured to the cooler Joseph was lifting out of the buggy. "I packed water, and Joe brought some bait, but we thought the tea would go good with our lunch."

Joseph grinned. *The one in the dark blue dress is Thelma all right.* Elma had worn a gray dress this morning. Since they hadn't dressed alike, it would be easier to tell them apart. "I hope you and your sister don't mind, but I brought Ginger along. She loves to go fishing with me and shouldn't be any problem at all."

"It's fine with me," Thelma spoke up.

Elma leaned down to pet the dog's head. "What a beautiful golden retriever."

"She's also very gentle and has been a great companion for me," Joseph said.

"I hope you'll enjoy what we brought to eat," Thelma said. "If not, then maybe the dog will eat it."

Elma rolled her eyes.

"I'm sure it'll be good." Joseph thumped his stomach. "Thinkin' about food makes me hungerich."

Delbert bumped Joseph's arm. "Let's get to fishin'. That oughta take your mind off your hungry stomach."

Joseph chuckled when his stomach growled in protest. "Sure hope so." He glanced over at the twins who were busy taking things out of their buggy. "Do you need any help?"

"I think maybe we do," Thelma said. "I have our picnic basket and a small cooler, and Elma brought two hefty tote bags along."

"That's right," Elma agreed. "In addition to blankets for us to sit on, I packed bug spray, sunglasses, umbrellas, a first-aid kit, plus a few other items."

Delbert frowned while swatting at the back of his neck, where a fly had landed. "How come you brought so much stuff? All we really need is the food, beverages, and fishing gear. Oh, and of course, my favorite fishing chair."

Elma's eyebrows shot up. "You brought your own chair?"

"Sure did." Delbert reached into the buggy and pulled out a canvas folding chair. "I always fish better when I'm sittin' on this."

Elma looked at the chair then quickly pulled a blanket out of one of the tote bags. "I'd rather sit on this."

"You don't say," Delbert was quick to reply.

Joseph pulled at his collar, which suddenly seemed too tight. Was he imagining it, or was there a bit of friction going on between his friend and Elma? He hoped that wasn't the case, because in order to keep seeing Thelma, he needed Delbert to go out with her twin.

Chapter 20

As Thelma sat on a log beside Joseph, holding her fishing pole, she looked over her shoulder and frowned. Elma sat on the blanket by herself, with a pen and crossword-puzzle magazine in her hand. *My sister will never get to know Delbert that way,* she fretted. He'd been kind enough to bring four poles and had even baited Elma's hook, but she showed no interest in fishing. *I need to think of something to get them together. Maybe when we eat lunch it'll go better.*

"By the way," Delbert said, looking at Thelma from where he sat on his chair. "If you and Elma still want me to fix your front porch, I'd be free to start on Monday."

"I believe we do. Isn't that right, Elma?" Thelma called to her sister.

"What was that?" Elma leaned slightly forward, putting the magazine down. "I was so engrossed in this puzzle that I didn't hear what was said."

"Delbert said he'd be free to start on our porch this coming Monday. We still want him to do the job, right?"

Elma nodded. "Definitely. It needs to be done, and soon."

"Great then. I'll be over early that morning."

"How early?" Elma asked. "We open the store at nine."

"I'll be there before then, in case you want to ask me any questions." Delbert looked at Thelma and smiled. "And if I have any questions, I'll come up to the store to speak with whichever of you isn't busy."

"That should work out fine," Thelma said.

"By the way..." Joseph moved a little closer to Thelma. Then Ginger got up and moved a little closer to Joseph, nudging his hand for some attention. "I keep forgetting to tell you that I enjoyed eating the cake you made for the charity event. It was sure tasty."

Thelma's face heated. "Danki, Joseph. I'm glad the way it looked didn't affect the taste."

"We never got to ask," Delbert said, "but how did the cake end up looking that way?"

"I had baked it the night before, and when I put the top layer on, one side looked lopsided," Thelma explained. "So to fix that problem, I added more frosting to one side of the top." She grimaced. "That may have been okay, but just then, our cat jumped up and got in the bowl of icing, so I couldn't use what was left. Then on the way to Shipshewana, our horse started acting up, lurching and lunging. I believe that's what made the cake look even worse."

"It was an embarrassment." Elma joined them at the pond's edge. "What I'd like to know, Delbert, is why you bid on our cake. I mean, lots of the other desserts looked much better than ours."

Delbert pointed at Joseph. "I did it for my good friend here. He wanted that cake and asked me to bid on it for him."

More than a little surprised, Thelma turned to face Joseph. "If you really wanted it, then why didn't you bid on it yourself?"

Joseph's ears turned pink, and so did his cheeks, making his freckles stand out. "I...uh...the thing is... I—I knew if I tried to call out a bid, I'd trip over my own t–tongue, like I'm doin' right now."

"But why did you want a lopsided cake?" Elma asked, lowering herself to the log beside Thelma.

Joseph dropped his gaze to the ground, rocking slightly back and forth. "I—I wanted to m–meet Thelma."

Thelma's eyes opened wide. She hardly knew what to

say. It made her feel good to know that Joseph had wanted to meet her, but to pay that much for their cake?

"And don't forget," Delbert said, "the cooking show was for a good cause."

"That's true," Elma agreed. "And we hope the proceeds from the auction brought in a lot of money."

"I don't know how much exactly, but I heard it was a success." Delbert's fishing pole jerked. He leaped to his feet. "I've got a bite, but I'm thinkin' it might be a sucker. If so, I'll throw it back in."

Thelma sat quietly, watching Delbert reel in his fish, unable to look at Joseph. He hadn't said a word since he'd announced that he'd asked his friend to bid on the cake so he could meet Thelma. She figured he was embarrassed, and she wished she could say something to make him feel better, but what? She couldn't blurt out that she was glad he'd wanted to meet her. Or was there something else she could say?

"Ginger is sure a nice dog. How long have you had her?" Thelma decided to ask.

"Six years already—since she was a puppy." Joseph looked tenderly at the dog. Thelma could tell they were true companions as Ginger laid her head in Joseph's lap. "After I bought my place two years before that, I missed having a dog around."

"She certainly is well behaved," Elma said.

He gave a nod. "Has been from the very beginning."

"Danki for inviting us to go fishing with you today." Leaning over, so she was closer to Joseph's ear, Thelma whispered, "I'm glad you asked Delbert to bid on the cake. If you hadn't, we wouldn't be sitting here right now, enjoying this lovely day."

He lifted his head and smiled at her. "Maybe we can do this again sometime. If not before winter sets in, then maybe come spring."

Thelma nodded. "I'd like that, Joseph." She knew now that he truly must be interested in her, or why would he have mentioned that?

Elma rose from her seat. "I think I'll go for a walk."

By now, Delbert had thrown the fish back in the pond and was about to put more bait on his hook when Joseph stood. "Why don't you go with her, Dell? It'll give you two a chance to get better acquainted. And take Ginger along. I think she could use some exercise."

"I suppose I may as well take a walk, since the good fish aren't biting anyway." Delbert turned to face Elma. "Should we go right or left?"

"Since you know the area and I don't, why don't you choose?" She smiled up at him.

"Let's head in this direction." Delbert pointed to the left.

Elma patted her leg. "Come on, Ginger!" The dog jumped up and came right over, her tail swishing about.

As Elma followed Delbert down a dirt path, she noticed several kinds of wildflowers. "Those are so *schee*."

Delbert stopped walking and turned to face her. "What's pretty?"

"Those." Elma pointed to the flowers.

"Ah, I see." He motioned to a pile of colored leaves. "I think those are equally *schee*."

Elma nodded. Apparently Delbert enjoyed the colors found in nature. It was nice to know they had that in common.

"How come you're not fishing today?" he asked as they continued walking.

"To be perfectly honest, I've never had that much interest in the sport. I enjoy eating some fish, but I don't have the patience to sit and wait for a fish to bite."

"It does take patience," he agreed. "But you know what they say: 'Good things come to those who wait.'"

Elma smiled in response.

"Don't know about you, but I'm about ready to eat. Should we head back so we can have lunch?"

"That's fine with me."

When they returned to the place where they'd left Joseph and Thelma, Elma was surprised to see how close they were sitting on that log. They both had their lines in the water and were chattering away like a pair of blue jays that had known each other for a long time.

"You're back so soon?" Thelma asked, looking up at Elma.

Delbert bobbed his head. "We decided it was time for lunch." He stood close to Joseph, and Ginger came and sat between them. "Have you caught anything yet?"

"No," Joseph replied, "but Thelma and I have been havin' a good conversation."

"I'm glad, but you can visit while we eat." Delbert opened his cooler. "I'll get out the beverages. Who wants a bottle of sweet tea?"

"I'll stick with water," Elma said as she spread the other blanket on the ground. She assumed she and Thelma would sit there and the men could share the blanket she'd sat on earlier.

But before she could make a move, Thelma knelt on the blanket closest to the picnic basket and began taking out the paper plates and napkins. Then Joseph, who had just finished putting Ginger's food out, plopped down right beside her.

"Is it okay if I sit here?" he asked.

"Of course." Thelma handed him a paper plate and passed a couple of others to Elma and Delbert, along with napkins.

Elma took the sandwiches from the cooler she and Thelma had brought and gave one to everyone. "I hope you like ham and cheese," she said. "We have some potato chips too."

"Ham and cheese sounds good to me." Delbert plopped his sandwich on the paper plate and plunked down in his folding chair, leaving Elma to sit on her blanket alone.

"Shall we pray?" Thelma suggested.

All heads bowed, and when their prayers ended, Delbert gave Elma a bottle of water. "What would you like, Thelma—water or sweet tea?"

"I think I'd like the tea."

"Oh Sister, there's a lot of *zucker* in one of those bottles. I've read the labels before and it—"

"Unless she has diabetes or something, a little sugar won't hurt her." Delbert handed Thelma some sweet tea. "How about you, Joe? What would you like to drink?"

"If there's enough sweet tea, I'll have one of those."

"No problem. I bought four bottles, thinkin' we'd each have one."

"If there were no zucker added, I might have taken one," Elma was quick to say. She didn't want Delbert to think she was ungrateful. She passed around the chips, veggies, and grapes to everyone.

As they ate, the twins talked about their grandparents' house and how much work it needed. "Sometimes it seems a bit overwhelming," Elma said, "but we've decided to take one project at a time."

"Come Monday, Delbert will be taking care of one of your problems," Joseph looked at Thelma. "If there are other things you need that don't involve carpentry, let me know. I'd be glad to help."

"Danki, we'll keep that in mind," Thelma responded.

When they finished with the sandwiches and other food, Thelma opened the wicker basket again and took out the cookies. "I hope you and Delbert like chocolate chip," she said, offering the cookies to Joseph. He took a couple and passed the container to Delbert.

Delbert grabbed one and held it up, his brows scrunching together. "They look like they're a bit burned on the bottom."

Thelma's face turned red. "Sorry about that. It's hard to judge how long things should bake in our old oven. It's a relic. Someday, if we start making enough money from the store, we hope to get a new stove."

"Our oven is heated with wood, not propane," Elma clarified.

"That explains everything." Delbert grunted. "I'll scrape off the dark part." He took out his fishing knife, poured some of his tea over it, wiped it on his trousers, and scraped away the dark part on the cookie.

Eww, Elma thought. *That really grosses me out.* She looked over at Thelma and discreetly pointed at Delbert's knife.

Thelma shrugged. Didn't this man's lack of manners bother her at all?

"That was a good meal, and I thank you for it." Delbert dropped the paper plate in a paper sack Elma had set out and rose to his feet. "Think I'll try my hand at fishin' again."

"I don't think that's such a good idea." Elma pointed to the darkening sky. "I felt a few raindrops, and it's likely to get worse."

Delbert waved his hand. "A few drops of rain won't hurt us. I can't leave here without getting at least one fish." He looked at Joseph. "How 'bout you? Aren't you gonna fish for a while too?"

Joseph looked at Thelma. "Do you want to fish some more?"

She smiled and nodded. "I'm in no hurry to go home."

"Okay, you three can fish, and I'll put our lunch basket away." Elma gathered everything up and got out her umbrella. She had a feeling these few drops of rain would soon become a full-blown rainstorm.

When more raindrops fell, Elma said she thought they should go.

"Let's wait and see how bad it gets." Delbert reached for some bait and was on the verge of putting it on his hook when a clap of thunder sounded. Everyone jumped, and Delbert hollered, "Ouch! I've got a fishhook stuck in my thumb!"

Chapter 21

Topeka

"Delbert's here," Thelma said, peering out the kitchen window. "He came early, like he said. The rig he came in today, Sister, is far more untidy than the one he had at the pond. Guess that's probably because this is Delbert's work buggy."

Elma, who had been folding a dish towel, joined Thelma at the window. "You're right. Guess I'd better go out and explain to him what needs to be done."

Thelma pressed her hands against her hips. "Delbert's a *schreiner*, Sister. I'm sure he knows what to do."

"Just because he's a carpenter doesn't mean he will know what we want to have done," Elma argued.

"I thought we already told him when he came to look at the saggy porch."

"We did, but I've thought of a couple other things since then." Elma grabbed her sweater and scooted out the door. She stepped onto the porch, being careful not to trip on any of the loose boards. She paused to breathe in the fresh autumn air. "Look at God's handiwork," she murmured. Everything from the golden leaves to the mixture of colorful mums filled her senses.

Elma watched Delbert unhook his horse from the rig and waited while he walked Snickers over to their corral. A few minutes later, Delbert joined her on the porch, carrying his tool belt. "Guder mariye," he said. "Beautiful morning, isn't it?"

"Good morning, and jah, I was taking it all in and

153

thinking the same thing. By the way, before I forget, how is your thumb?"

He held up his hand. "Still hurts a bit, but it'll be fine with the bandage I'm wearing."

"I hope you put some disinfectant on it after you got home Saturday."

He nodded. "I've got more stuff in my work buggy, so as soon as I take it out, I'll get busy on your porch."

"Before you get started, I wanted to point something out." Elma motioned to the handrail. "In addition to the boards in the porch floor, I'd like that replaced too."

He looked at her quizzically. "Are you sure? It looks like it's still in fairly good shape."

She shook her head. "No, it's not. See, right there, some of the wood is beginning to split."

Delbert leaned down and studied the area she was referring to. "Hmm... I can probably fix that with some putty and wood glue."

"I'd rather it be replaced."

He shrugged. "Okay, if that's what you want. Anything else?"

"I do have a few other tasks in mind, but maybe you should get this project done first." Elma was about to step back inside, when she thought of something else. "Thelma and I will be at the store most of the day, but we'll leave the front door unlocked so you can go in to use the bathroom or get a drink of water. One of us will come up to the house around noon to fix you some lunch."

"There's no need for that," he said. "I brought my own lunch along."

"Okay. I'll see you later then." With a quick smile, she went back into the house.

It was getting close to noon and Delbert was thinking about stopping for lunch, when Elma showed up. He knew it was her because she'd been wearing a dark maroon dress when she'd spoken to him earlier.

"How's it going?" she asked, moving toward the porch steps.

"It's going okay, but you'd better not come up here." He motioned to the boards he'd pried loose. "Oh, and I'm afraid I've got bad news."

Her forehead creased. "What's that?"

"You have a problem with carpenter ants."

"Oh dear." Elma clasped her hand over her mouth. "How bad is it?"

"Pretty bad." Delbert gestured from one end of the porch to the other. "They're about everywhere, I'm afraid." He lifted his hammer and smacked a big black ant crawling near his boot.

"I wonder how they got into the porch."

"Carpenter ants build their nests in wood, so they're often found in and around homes. They don't actually eat the wood, but they bore through the wood, making a place for their nest."

"Oh. So maybe that's not so bad."

"It can be. Carpenter ants can find their way into your home and even get into your food and water sources, so they need to be taken care of." He smacked another crawling bug. "Have you seen any sign of them in the house?"

Elma shook her head and mumbled something about a rat and some mice.

"You've got a rodent problem too?"

Her face flamed. "We did, but our katze have taken care of that." Wrinkles formed above her brows. "What are we supposed to do about the ants?"

"The first thing will be to kill them off. You could call a professional company to come out and do that, but it'll be expensive, and they might not get out here right away."

"Would you be able to get rid of the ants?" she asked.

He nodded. "I can get some bait from the hardware store to lure them out, then trail 'em back to the nest so I can figure out exactly where they're hiding."

"Can you do it without using anything toxic? My

folks have always tried to use organic methods, even when dealing with bugs and other critters that have invaded our garden. All natural is better than taking the chance of poisoning a pet or any kinner that may be playing in the yard."

Reaching under his straw hat, Delbert scratched his head. "How often do you have children in your yard?"

"Well, maybe not here, but they do come to the store with their parents, and if one were to wander down to the house, then. . ."

Delbert lifted his hands in defeat. "Okay, I get it. I'll make sure to use tamper-resistant bait stations."

"Will it be toxic?"

"Jah, but it'll be safer because—"

"Is there anything natural you can try?" she questioned.

"I've used a boric acid bait before. I'll mix one-third powdered sugar with two-thirds boric acid, fill some bottle caps with the mixture, and set it down around the areas where I've seen the ants. When they return the next time, it will kill the ants that are already in the nest. See, the boric acid penetrates the insect's body and dissolves in there."

Elma wrinkled her nose. "That sounds ekelhaft."

"It may be disgusting, but if it gets rid of your ant problem without using poison, then you oughta be glad." He stepped off the porch. "Unless you have some boric acid here, I'd better run into town to get some."

"I'm sure we don't have any of that, but we do have some powdered sugar."

"Great. If you'll have that sitting out for me, I'll mix up the stuff when I get back."

"I'll make sure it's ready. I'll leave the powdered sugar on the kitchen counter. Until you get the porch finished, my sister and I will only use the back door."

"That's a good idea. See you later then," Delbert called over his shoulder as he headed for his horse and buggy.

When Delbert came back an hour and a half later, he found a box of powdered sugar and a large measuring cup on the kitchen counter with a note attached, telling him what it was for. "Like I needed that," Delbert mumbled. "Does she think I'm *dumm*?"

Grasping the note, he read it out loud. "Before you leave for the day could you please come up to the store? There is something else I'd like you to do."

"What does she want now? I'm not even done with the porch."

Delbert wondered whether Elma was always so demanding or if she had singled him out. Maybe demanding wasn't the right word. Elma was a little too opinionated to suit Delbert. She reminded him of his ex-girlfriend, Mattie, who'd wanted to make Delbert become the kind of man she thought he should be. Her constant suggestions and opinions about what he should or shouldn't do had caused him to finally break things off and give up on marriage. Of course, having put up with five somewhat bossy older sisters when he was growing up hadn't helped either. But Delbert thought he ought to at least give Elma a chance, since Joseph was set on establishing a relationship with Thelma and wanted him to be a part of the foursome. He'd give her the benefit of the doubt and see what happened. After all, she was pretty cute.

Delbert's nose twitched and he sneezed. He went to the sink to get a drink and sneezed a few more times. *Achoo! Achoo! Achoo!* He reached for a paper towel and wiped his nose as his eyes began to water.

Meow! Meow!

Delbert looked down and scowled at the cat rubbing against his leg. No wonder he'd sneezed. "Go on, get!" he said, moving to one side.

The cat followed, meowing up at him as though it wanted something. Whatever it was, the feline wouldn't get it from Delbert. He was allergic to cats and couldn't get anywhere near one without his nose acting up. Sometimes when his allergies got real bad, he would become so stuffed up he could barely breathe. He wasn't going to stay in here any longer. He needed to get back outside.

"I've done as much on your porch as I can for today," Delbert said when he entered the twins' store. "I need to be in Shipshe soon to bid on another job."

"Oh, before you go," Elma said, "there's something else my sister and I would like to have done."

"You said something about that in your note." Delbert pulled out his hanky and wiped his nose.

"Do you have a cold?" Elma asked, stepping out from behind the counter where she stood with her twin sister.

"Nope. I'm allergic to *katze.*"

"There's no cat in here," Thelma spoke up. "Although we probably will bring the *busslin* out when it's time to find them all homes."

Delbert grimaced. "Kittens? Do you have kittens in your house? I thought it was just the one cat."

"What one cat?" Elma asked. "Were you in the basement? That's where the kittens and mama cat are."

Delbert shook his head. "I was in the kitchen getting a drink when this orange-and-white cat rubbed against my trousers. It made me sneeze." If there were more cats in the basement, he wouldn't go down there.

Thelma pressed her fingers to her lips. "Uh-oh. I must have forgotten to put Tiger out this morning. I'd better do that right now, before he makes a mess in the house." She slipped past Elma and rushed out the door.

Delbert moved across the room and leaned on the counter. "What else are you wantin' me to do?"

"There's a piece of fabric hanging below the kitchen sink. Thelma and I would like to have it replaced with real wooden doors." Elma smiled—that oh so sweet smile that made him feel like he couldn't say anything but yes.

"It's in the kitchen, huh?"

"That's what I just said."

He paused to blow his nose then returned his hanky to his pocket. "Will the cat be in there when I'm workin'?"

"Oh no, I'll make sure he's not."

"That's good, 'cause if he were, I'd probably have to wear a dust mask so I wouldn't have to breathe all that cat dander." Delbert paused to rub his eyes.

"I'm sorry you were exposed to Tiger. We'll make sure it doesn't happen again."

Delbert coughed then smiled. "Okay. When did you want me to start on the cabinet doors?"

"There's no real rush. Whenever you finish with the porch. And if you have work for other people that needs to be done first, that's all right too."

"I'll get it done as soon as I can." Delbert glanced to his left and noticed a rack full of candy. "Got any jelly beans over there?" he asked, gesturing to the candy.

"I believe so," Elma replied, "but I'm not sure how fresh they are. Thelma and I are still in the process of taking inventory of all the stock in our store. We haven't done the candy rack yet."

"Think I'll go have a look-see anyhow." Delbert strode over to the candy and plucked off a package of mixed jelly beans. The black licorice–flavored ones looked especially enticing. "I'll take these. How much do I owe you?" he asked, plopping the bag on the counter.

"Let me see if there's an expiration date on them." She picked up the bag and slipped on her reading glasses. It seemed odd to Delbert that a young woman her age would have a need for reading glasses. Come to think of it, he wasn't sure how old she and her sister were. In the few times they'd been together, the subject hadn't come up. Delbert guessed they were probably in their mid to late twenties. He thought about asking Elma her age, but a customer had entered the store, and she looked like she wanted to ask Elma a question.

"So how much for the jelly beans?" he quickly asked.

She pressed her lips together, staring at the package. "You know, Delbert, eating too much zucker is bad for your health."

Delbert's fingers curled into a ball, biting into his palms. Did Elma think she was his mother? One minute she could be so nice, then the next, she was downright irritating. Making no reference to her comment, he said, "How much do they cost?"

"Since you seem determined to have them, and since the expiration date was three months ago, I'll give you the jelly beans for free."

"Really?"

She nodded.

"Danki. I'll be back sometime tomorrow to finish the porch." He picked up the bag of candy and headed for the door, feeling a little better toward Elma than he had before. Now that he knew they sold jelly beans in this store, he'd make sure to visit more often.

Chapter 22

LaGrange

"Are you ready for a rousing game of Ping-Pong?" Joseph asked when he arrived at Delbert's on Friday night.

Delbert grinned. "More to the point, are you ready to lose?"

"We'll have to wait and see about that." Joseph removed his jacket and hung it over the back of a chair.

"Should we get started now, or did you want a cup of coffee first?" Delbert asked. "I've got a pot heatin' on the stove."

"Maybe I will have a cup." Joseph followed Delbert into the kitchen and took a seat at the table, while Delbert got out the mugs and poured the coffee. "Sure was a colorful week, with autumn leaves at their peak."

"You're right, and this is my favorite time of the year." Delbert glanced out the window and yawned. "You want a cinnamon roll?"

"Did you bake 'em?"

Delbert shook his head. "I've been too busy this week to do any baking." He handed Joseph a cup and placed several cinnamon rolls on the table.

"Busy workin' in your shop? Or workin' on somebody's home?"

"I worked at my shop a few days, but the rest of the week I was in Topeka, at the Hochstetler twins' place."

Joseph set his cup down and plopped his elbows on the table, eager to hear about the twins—especially

Thelma. "How'd it go over there?" He helped himself to a roll.

"I got their porch done, and then I made a couple of doors for under the kitchen sink."

"Sounds like you've been busy."

"Jah."

"Did you see Thelma?"

Delbert grabbed a cinnamon roll, broke it in half, and dunked the piece in his hot coffee. "Not so much. Saw a lot of Elma though."

Joseph smiled, biting into the soft, sweet pastry. "That's good to hear."

Delbert shook his head. "No, not really." He finished up his last piece of the cinnamon roll.

"Seeing Elma isn't good?" Joseph couldn't hide his confusion. "But you said before that you thought she was pretty." He took a sip of his steaming hot coffee.

"She is, but she doesn't like to fish, and on top of that, she sometimes gets on my nerves."

"Oh really? Why's that?" Joseph blew on the coffee.

Delbert reached for another roll. "She says things to irritate me and offers her opinion on how I should do things. No wonder she's not married."

"I wouldn't talk about who's not married, if I were you. In case you haven't looked in the mirror lately, you're over thirty and still not sportin' a beard."

Delbert jerked his head around to meet Joseph's gaze. "That's right. I'm still single, and I kinda like it that way." He took another bite of the pastry he held.

Joseph leaned forward. "Are you sure? Don't you think havin' a wife and family would be nice?"

Delbert just drank down his coffee and grabbed another cinnamon roll.

"Maybe you're too set in your ways."

"That could be." Delbert pushed away from the table, licking some of the icing that had stuck to his fingers. "I'd best go wash my hands." He got up and went to the sink. After he'd washed and dried his hands, he returned to the table. "Are you ready to play that game of table tennis now?"

"Not quite. I haven't finished my coffee yet." Truth was, Joseph felt like he and Delbert were already playing a type of ping-pong.

Delbert went to the stove and got a refill then sat back down.

"I've been thinking that maybe we could see if Thelma and Elma would like to come over to my house for pizza next Friday night. We could play a few board games after we eat."

"I don't think so, Joe. Elma gets on my nerves. She even made an issue of me eating jelly beans the other day." Delbert grimaced. "Made me feel like a little boy being scolded for having too much candy."

"You should take that as a good sign."

Delbert's eyebrows pulled together. "Good sign of what?"

"That she likes you and cares about your welfare. Too much zucker can be bad, you know."

"I don't eat too much sugar. Besides, she's not with me all the time, so there's no way she can know how much sugar I eat." Delbert folded his arms. "If you want to keep seeing Thelma, that's fine by me, but I think I'm done pursuing Elma."

Joseph sat rigidly in his chair as a sense of panic set in. "Aw, come on, Dell. You don't know Elma all that well yet. I think you need to give her a chance."

Delbert slowly shook his head. "I don't know about that."

Joseph leaned closer to Delbert. "Won't you go out with her a couple more times, even if it's only as a friend? I want to keep seeing Thelma, and I really need you with me."

"You don't need me in order to see Thelma."

"Jah, I do, because I still feel a little awkward and

tongue-tied when I'm around her. Besides, after you get to know Elma a little better, maybe you'll decide that she's the right girl for you." Joseph's stomach tightened. If Delbert gave up on seeing Elma, he didn't know what he would do. Could he really find the courage to court Thelma on his own?

Delbert sighed. "I'll give it some thought. Now are we gonna play Ping-Pong or what?"

"Sure, and if you wanna serve first, that's fine by me."

Topeka

"Did you happen to notice that the FOR SALE sign is back on the house across the street?" Elma took a seat in her favorite chair. "The sign did read SALE PENDING before. I wonder what happened with the potential buyers. It's such a nice place too."

"That's right. I thought the family from Graybill was interested in getting that house." Thelma shifted a bit on Grandpa's old chair. "I guess it wasn't meant to be. When the time is right, maybe someone else will buy the house."

"What are you knitting?" Elma asked, noticing Thelma's yarn. "It doesn't look like gloves for Mom. The yarn is a different color."

"No, it's not. I finished those several days ago." Thelma held up the ball of blue yarn. "I'm making a stocking cap for Joseph."

"Really?" Elma placed the dress she was hemming in her lap. "Are you serious about him? I mean, you've only gone out with him a few times."

"I know, but I really like Joe. I may give him the cap for Christmas."

"What do we have here, Sister—a case of love at first sight, the way it was for Mom and Dad?"

Thelma's heart raced a bit, and she felt the heat of a blush. "Maybe, but I'm not sure how he feels about me."

"If the dreamy-eyed look he gets when he's with you

is any indication, then I'd say you have nothing to worry about." Elma grinned and picked up her mending.

Thelma smiled in response, feeling relaxed. "How about you and Delbert? He's been over here quite a bit in the last week, and it seemed like you were talking to him a lot."

Elma sighed. "I don't think he likes me, Thelma."

Thelma's eyes widened. "What makes you say that?"

"He seems irritated whenever I ask him a question."

"He was probably preoccupied. After all, he did come here to work."

Elma threaded her needle. "I know, but it was more than that. I just feel that we don't communicate well or really have much in common."

"Dad and Mom don't have a lot of things in common, but they've been happily married for thirty-four years."

"Can we change the subject?" She stood. "It's getting chilly in here. Think I'll throw another log on the fire."

"Want me to do that so you can keep working on your new dress? You'll probably want to wear it to church this Sunday."

"You're right. I do. And if you're sure you don't mind, it would be nice if you put the next log on the fire."

"I don't mind at all." Thelma set her knitting aside and crossed the room. She'd picked up a piece of wood when she heard a loud *meow*. "Uh-oh. I'll bet that's Tiger. I forgot to let him in this evening. And by the way, I found a good-sized box in the back of the store earlier today. It's perfect for Misty and her growing kittens. Before long, we'll be able to take them out to the store to try and find them new homes. I hope you won't mind, but I'd like to keep one of Misty's kittens."

Elma wrinkled her nose. "Another cat? Oh Sister, don't you think we have enough of those already?"

"Maybe, but they do keep the mice down."

"True."

"I've grown attached to the little cuties but mostly

the white-colored female in the group." Thelma yearned to keep the kitten.

"Okay. I guess one more katz won't matter. As you said, having the katze keeps down the mice. But one thing to consider is that Delbert is allergic to cats. We can't allow Tiger in the house when Delbert is here, but it'll just be till he's done working for us."

"I thought he was done. He fixed the front porch and put the doors under the kitchen sink. Isn't that all you asked him to do?"

"At first it was, but then I asked if he would fix the loose railing going upstairs to the bedrooms, and I'm thinking we may want him to replace the broken lock on the kitchen window. There's also that door upstairs that catches."

Thelma smiled. "I'm thinking from your expression that you're worried about Delbert. Does that mean you like him a lot?"

"I can't say that. I don't want him having an allergic attack when he's trying to work on our house."

"He won't be coming here tonight, so I'm gonna let Tiger in." Thelma tossed the wood on the fire and opened the front door. She hoped things would work out between her sister and Delbert, because if Elma didn't have a man friend, then Thelma wouldn't either. It wouldn't be fair, and besides, she'd made that childhood promise not to get married unless Elma was too.

Chapter 23

"I am sure looking forward to this evening," Thelma said as she and Elma climbed into their buggy the next Friday. "It'll be fun to see where Joseph lives and spend the evening with him and Delbert."

Elma sighed. "I suppose, although I was honestly looking forward to a restful evening at home. It's been a busy week at the store, and I'm tired." She picked up the reins and got Pearl moving. "Brr. . . You can tell it's November, even though it's only the first week."

"If the night air doesn't do it, I'll bet you'll perk up as soon as we eat and play a few board games. I know how much you enjoy the competition."

"That's true. A good game of Rook or Settlers is always fun." She yawned. "I hope you're not planning to stay too late."

Thelma touched Elma's arm. "We can go whenever you like. Just say the word and I'll be ready to head for home."

Elma had a feeling that wouldn't turn out to be the case. Knowing her sister, they'd probably be there until quite late, since Thelma liked to socialize. *I hope she doesn't get any ideas about the two of us doing some silly skit tonight.* Thelma had always enjoyed putting on skits when they got together with a group of friends or attended some family function. Elma always went along with it because she didn't want people to think she was a poor sport or too serious about things. Tonight though, with two men they were getting to know, Elma wouldn't feel comfortable try-ing to make Delbert and Joseph laugh by acting out one of the skits they'd done in the past.

Clucking at Pearl, Elma watched as the steam blew from the horse's nostrils when she picked up a little more speed. *Maybe if we keep busy playing board games, the subject of skits won't come up.*

LaGrange

"Yum. Those pizzas baking in my oven sure smell good," Joseph said to Delbert as they worked together at setting the table. "Danki for helping me make them."

"Not a problem," Delbert replied. "I'm happy to do it."

"You know your way around the kitchen a lot better than I do." Joseph placed four glasses on the table and glanced at the clock on the far wall.

"Living on your own as long as you've been, I would have thought you'd be a pro by now." Delbert enjoyed teasing his friend.

"You'd sure think so, wouldn't you?" Shrugging his shoulders, Joseph looked toward the window. "I was expecting Thelma and Elma to be here by now. Hope they don't have any trouble finding my place. Since it's the only house on this road that looks like a log cabin, it shouldn't be too hard to find."

"It's a crisp, clear night, so if you gave them good directions, they shouldn't have a problem." Delbert thumped Joseph's back. "Try not to worry."

"I've been looking forward to this all week, and I want everything to go right."

"You're one big bundle of nerves. It'll be fine. You'll see." Delbert gestured around the room. "You got the place all clean and tidy, so relax."

Joseph smiled. "By the way, danki for agreeing to get together with Elma again. I think it should be a relaxing evening for all of us."

"If things don't go well tonight, you're gonna owe me big—maybe another meal out at my favorite restaurant." Delbert chuckled as he went to get the hot pepper flakes from the refrigerator. He wasn't so sure this evening would be relaxing but looked forward to eating that pepperoni pizza and drinking a tall glass of the cold cider he'd brought along. Thelma had left a message for Joseph, accepting the supper invitation and saying that she and Elma would bring a dessert. He hoped it would be something he liked and not more overly baked cookies.

Why can't Elma be more laid back like her sister? he wondered. *She always seems so uptight. It gets on my nerves when she's so free with her opinion. Joseph's lucky to have found a girl like Thelma.*

"I think they may be here. I heard a horse whinny outside." Joseph went to the window to look out.

Delbert laughed. "I sure hope it was outside."

"Very funny." Joseph opened the back door. "I'll go take care of their horse."

After Joseph went outside, Delbert opened the oven door and checked on the pizza. It was a good thing Elma and Thelma were here, because the pizza was almost done. *Probably should've waited till they showed up to bake the pizza,* he told himself, *but I figured they'd be here before now.*

Delbert closed the oven door and turned the oven down. Then he went to the refrigerator and took out the tossed green salad he'd also made, placing it on the table.

One of the twins entered the kitchen. "Good evening, Delbert. The pizza smells good." She stepped up to the stove. "I don't mean to sound envious, but I wish we had an oven like yours."

"I'm sure it's a challenge to use your old woodstove for cooking." He stood by the table, holding the pot holders.

"Jah," she said, holding out a container. "Here are some pumpkin whoopie pies I picked up at the bakery today, since neither Thelma nor I had time to do any baking this week."

"That's great." Delbert now knew that he was talking to Elma. "You can set them over there on the counter." His mouth watered, thinking about how good those cookies were going to taste. "Pumpkin's one of my favorite kinds of whoopie pies. Course I like chocolate, banana, and lemon too. Anything sweet and it's all right by me."

Elma set the container down and turned to face him. "You certainly have a sweet tooth, don't you?"

"Guess I do." He put the pot holders away.

"Have you ever considered how much damage all that sugar can do to your body?"

He shrugged. "Nope, sure haven't."

"Well, maybe you should."

Delbert grunted. If this was what he could expect all evening, he might go home early instead of spending the night at Joseph's like he'd planned. They were going fishing on Saturday and he had brought his fishing gear along, but they could always meet in the morning. Joseph had suggested they invite the twins again, but Delbert talked him out of it, saying he thought they'd get more fishing done if it was just the two of them.

"What kind of pizza did you make?" Elma asked.

Delbert opened the oven door. "It's ready, so I hope Thelma and Joseph come in soon."

She bent down to observe the pizza. "Is that pepperoni?"

"Yep. It's Joe's and my favorite kind."

She wrinkled her nose. "Is that the only topping you have?"

"What's wrong? Don't you like pepperoni?" He turned off the oven and closed the door.

"To be honest, it's not one of my favorites."

"Sorry about that. When Thelma told Joe she liked pepperoni, I figured with you being twins that you would too."

"We may look alike and enjoy some of the same things, but we're not identical in every sense of the word."

"What kind of pizza do you like?" he asked, studying the curve of her pretty face.

"I really enjoy a vegetarian pizza, but plain cheese is okay too."

Delbert motioned to the bowl he'd set on the table. "There's plenty of salad, so maybe you can fill up on that."

She offered him a quick smile. "Maybe I will try one piece of pizza, since Joseph worked so hard making it for us."

Delbert leaned against the cupboard and folded his arms. "Actually, I did most of the work. Joe's not much of a cook, so he asked me to help him make the pizza."

Her eyes widened. "I—I didn't realize that. I'll definitely try a piece then."

Just then the back door creaked as it opened, and Joseph and Thelma stepped in, both smiling from ear to ear. *Those two are obviously crazy about each other,* Delbert mused. *I have a feeling by next year at this time my good friend may be growing a baart.* He stroked his own chin. *Wonder how I'd look wearin' a beard.*

As they sat around the table a short time later, Elma found herself enjoying the meal. The salad was delicious, with lots of cut-up veggies in it, as well as green lettuce leaves. She had to admit that even the pizza was pretty good. Of course, she picked off the pieces of pepperoni and fed them to Joseph's dog, who lay under the table. While she didn't care much for cats, Elma did have a soft spot for dogs—especially one as pretty as Ginger.

"Would you like to try some of this crushed pepper to sprinkle on your next slice of pizza?" Delbert asked, looking at the twins. "It adds a little kick to—"

Before he could finish his sentence, Elma took the bottle and shook a fair amount on.

"You may want to—"

Eagerly taking a bite, Elma felt the heat rise from her throat as she swallowed the piece of pizza. An uncontrollable cough started as she tried to catch her breath, while tears flowed down her cheeks.

"Here, Sister, drink some of this." Thelma handed Elma a cup of cider.

After Elma drank some of the cold cider, she looked at Delbert and frowned. "You should have warned me that it was so hot."

"Tried, but you put those hot pepper sprinkles on so fast. By the time you took a bite, it was too late." Delbert picked up his napkin and fanned Elma's face with it, which only made her more irritated. "You only have to use a little of that stuff to enhance the flavor of the pizza. Are you all right now?" he asked.

"I'll be fine." Elma brushed the flakes off the rest of her pizza. Glancing to her left where Delbert sat, Elma noticed that he had a glob of cheese stuck to his chin. Wondering if she should say anything, she kept staring at him.

"What's wrong?" Delbert asked, sprinkling a little more pepper on his pizza. "Why are you lookin' at me so strangely? Are you waiting for me to choke?"

Before she could say anything, Joseph snickered and pointed at Delbert's chin.

Delbert swiped his hand across it, leaving the sticky cheese on his fingers. Everyone laughed. It was then that Elma saw a splotch of pizza sauce on Delbert's shirt, but she decided not to mention it. If someone else did, that was one thing, but she didn't want to seem overly critical. She wouldn't have minded getting back at Delbert after choking on the hot pepper, but in truth, it was her own fault. For Thelma's sake, she needed to be on her best behavior this evening.

"Say, I was wondering, Delbert, would you have the time to stain our barn before winter sets in?" Elma asked.

He added more salad to his plate. "Sure, that shouldn't be a problem."

"Maybe I'll come along and lend a hand," Joseph was

quick to say. "With two of us working, the barn will get done faster."

Thelma smiled. "That would be great. We'll pay you both of course."

Joseph shook his head. "There's no need for that. You can pay Delbert if you want to, but I'm more than happy to do it for free."

Delbert cast Joseph a quick glance. He shrugged and said, "Guess I can do the same."

After they finished the meal and the dishes were done, Joseph brought out a couple of games. "What should we play first?" he asked. "Uno or Rook?"

"I vote for Uno," Thelma said.

Joseph looked over at her and smiled. "That's what it'll be then. Unless Dell and Elma don't want to play that."

"I think we should let our supper settle a bit and then eat dessert," Elma said.

Thelma and Joseph bobbed their heads, but Delbert's forehead wrinkled. He looked disappointed. Joseph didn't seem to notice though, as he shuffled the cards and dealt, placing the cards facedown. The rest of them he put facedown in the center of the table. Then he turned one card over so the game could begin.

"You go first, Thelma," he said, "since you're sitting to my left."

Thelma picked up her cards and studied them. "I don't have a card to match the color or number of the one you laid down, so I guess it's my sister's turn."

"Don't forget to draw a card," Elma reminded.

"Oh, that's right." Thelma drew a card off the pile in the center of the table.

Then Elma took her turn and discarded one of her cards. Delbert played a reverse card, so it was Elma's turn again.

The game continued, until Elma had one card left. "Uno!" she shouted.

Delbert looked at her suspiciously. "Already? We haven't been playing that long."

She stiffened. "I hope you're not accusing me of cheating."

"Course not," he said, shaking his head. "I was merely making a statement."

On Elma's next turn, she laid down a wild card, her last one.

Thelma moaned. "I still have seven cards left."

"I have five." Joseph looked at Delbert. "How many do you have?"

Delbert tossed his cards on the table. "Too many, and it's all because somebody kept playing 'draw two' cards that were meant for me." He looked at Elma.

"Sorry," she mumbled. "I had to play the cards I had."

"Let's play again." Joseph gathered up the cards and handed them to Thelma. She shuffled and dealt, and the game started. This time Delbert won.

Elma won the next game and Delbert the game after that.

Thelma looked at Joseph. "I think we're both losing this game."

"It doesn't matter," he said, smiling at her. "It's fun for us all to be together." Pushing his chair back, he stood. "Maybe we oughta have some dessert now. Who wants coffee to go with the whoopie pies?"

All hands shot up.

"Do you need some help?" Thelma asked.

"Sure, you can set out the whoopies," he replied.

"I'll bring in another log for the fireplace." Delbert pushed back his chair then jumped when Ginger let out a *yip*. "Sorry, girl. I didn't see you behind my chair." He bent down to pet the dog's head.

"You have to watch when there's a pet in the house," Elma said. "They can get underfoot without you even knowing it."

"I'm sure Ginger knows I didn't do it on purpose."

Delbert headed for the door without putting on a jacket.

While Joseph and Thelma got things ready, Elma tried to think of something to say when Delbert came back with the wood. She probably shouldn't have said anything when Joseph's dog yipped. Without a doubt, she felt uncomfortable around him tonight. More so than the other times they'd been together. Was there the remotest possibility that they could become a couple?

Chapter 24

"That was such a nice evening, wasn't it?" Joseph said after the twins left. "Thelma is fun to be with. Some of the jokes she told had me laughing so hard my sides ached."

"She was pretty funny," Delbert agreed. "I wish Elma were more like her."

Joseph's eyebrows shot up. "You're interested in Thelma?"

"I didn't say I was interested in her. Said I wished Elma were more like her."

"So you're not interested in Thelma?"

Delbert shook his head and thumped Joseph's shoulder. "Don't look so *naerfich*. I'm not gonna steal your *aldi*."

"Whew, that's a relief! I wasn't nervous, but I'll admit, you had me worried there for a minute." Joseph released a deep breath. "I do think of Thelma as my girlfriend now."

Delbert snickered. "I kind of got that impression. Now don't do anything to mess it up."

Joseph winced. "Did I say or do something wrong tonight?"

"Not that I know of. You and Thelma seemed to get along fine." Delbert grimaced. "I, on the other hand, had a few issues with Elma."

"Really? I thought everything was going okay. What kind of issues did you have with her?"

"For one thing, when we were playing the last game of the night, Elma made a big deal out of me not drinking my coffee before it got cold." Delbert talked in a high-pitched tone, trying to imitate Elma's voice. " 'Oh Delbert, aren't you going to drink your coffee? It's probably cold by now.'"

"Guess I didn't hear her say that," Joseph said. "What'd you say?"

"I said, 'Maybe I like it cold.'" Delbert shifted in his chair. "Oh, and when we were playing the games, Elma was very competitive."

"And you weren't?"

Delbert shrugged. "Maybe a little. I've never met a woman who acted that way when it came to playing a game."

"Everyone's different, and some people take their game playing more seriously. Look how Elma choked on the hot pepper flakes you suggested she use on her pizza. Maybe you should have explained it before handing her the bottle."

"Guess that's true. But she took it so fast and then took a bite even faster. I had no time to warn her." Delbert rose from his chair, abruptly changing the subject. "I don't know about you, but I'm bushed. Think I'll head to bed. See you in the morning."

Joseph gave a nod. "I'll be up bright and early."

"Are you feeling all right? You're awfully quiet," Thelma said as she and Elma traveled home from Joseph's. Thelma was driving Pearl, since Elma said she didn't feel like it.

"I'm tired, and I've got the beginning of a koppweh."

"Oh no. I hope it's not another migraine coming on."

"It's not bad yet," Elma responded. "I'm sure with some aspirin and a good night's rest I'll feel better in the morning."

Thelma reached across the seat and patted her sister's arm. "Did you enjoy yourself tonight?"

"It was fun playing games, but I think Delbert was upset that I won so often."

"Most men are competitive. He probably couldn't deal with losing to a woman." Thelma smiled. "Delbert's sure a lot different than Joseph. Joe always seems so easygoing."

"That's true," Elma agreed. "You're lucky to have found him."

"I think it's more that he found me. But then, Delbert found you as well."

"Humph! Well, the least he could have done was warn me about those pepper flakes in time. I thought I would choke to death, it was so hot."

"In Delbert's defense, you did take the bottle from him rather fast, and you put an awful lot of the stuff on your pizza," Thelma said. "I think he was getting ready to warn you, but you didn't give him much of a chance. You bit into that pizza so quickly, even I was surprised."

"I was only trying to show Delbert that I was receptive to his suggestion."

"In any event, I don't think the evening was a total flop, do you?"

Elma shrugged as she sat quietly beside Thelma.

"You seemed to enjoy petting Joe's dog tonight," Thelma commented.

"Jah. Ginger's a nice *hund*."

"She seems to have taken to you as well."

Elma laughed. "That's probably because I was feeding her pieces of pepperoni under the table."

Thelma gasped. "You did that?"

"Didn't you notice?"

"No, can't say that I did."

"Probably because your focus was on Joseph all night."

Do I detect a bit of jealousy in my sister's tone? Thelma wondered. *If she and Delbert would set their differences aside and focus on each other's positive qualities, they could have a nice relationship too. Sure wish I could say or do something to make that happen.*

Topeka

When Elma woke up the following morning, she knew there was no way she could work in the store, because her head pulsated with pain. It was even worse than the night before. It wouldn't be good to put the CLOSED sign in the window, like they had on the Saturday they'd gone fishing with Delbert and Joseph. They had quickly discovered that for some folks in their community, Saturday was the only day they could shop. *I wonder if Thelma could handle things by herself.*

Elma forced herself to climb out of bed and went into the hall to knock on Thelma's bedroom door. She hoped her sister hadn't already gone downstairs, because given the way her head pounded and her stomach felt nauseous, she would need help making her way down those stairs to the bathroom. She'd just made it to Thelma's door when it opened and Thelma stepped out. "Oh Sister, I didn't know you were standing there. Are you all right? You don't look so well."

"My headache is worse than it was last night," Elma explained, "and I don't think I can work at the store today."

"It's okay," Thelma assured her. "I'll manage on my own. You should go rest on the sofa so you don't have to go up and down the stairs today."

"Are you sure? Maybe we should close the store."

Thelma shook her head. "As you have said many times, we need the money. Besides, if we close, any people coming in today will be disappointed."

"You're right. I feel bad about leaving you all alone to run the store, but I don't have it in me this morning to work."

Thelma patted Elma's arm gently. "I'll be fine, and if things get too crazy, I'll close up early."

"If I feel better before the day is out, I'll come out to the store." Elma gave her sister a hug.

Thelma had only been at the store fifteen minutes when Mary came by with little Richard and Philip. Thelma smiled when the boys plopped down on the braided rug near the children's books. Each of them picked out a book while their mother did her shopping. She was glad to see that Richard's arm had healed and he was no longer wearing a cast. "Would you like a piece of candy?" she asked, holding out a small chocolate bar for each of them. The brothers nodded and eagerly took the candy. "Danki," they said.

Once more, Thelma found herself longing to be a mother. *If Joseph and I got married, I wonder what our children would look like. Would they have his red hair and freckles, or would they resemble me?* She shook her head. *I need to get back to work and quit daydreaming about Joe. He may not even be entertaining the idea of marriage.* The words of Proverbs 16:20 that she'd read in Grandma's Bible and committed to memory came to mind. "I need to trust You, Lord," she whispered.

All morning Thelma was busy at the store, but by noon things had slowed down. Without customers for the moment, she decided to put the CLOSED sign in the window and go check on Elma. She was just getting ready to do that, when Elma showed up.

"How's it going?" they asked in unison.

Thelma laughed. "A few minutes ago it was real busy in here. How are you feeling right now?"

"Much better." Elma lifted the basket she held. "I brought lunch out for us, and I'm ready to help you here for the rest of the day."

"Danki for that. I've been having hunger pangs for the last hour or so."

"Why don't we go to the back room to eat, since there's a table and chairs in there. If someone comes into the store, I'm sure we'll hear them."

"Sounds good to me."

Elma moved toward the counter and pointed to a stack of material. "Is this here for a reason?"

"It was left from the fabric I cut for Mary Lambright. I got too busy to put it away."

"What about these?" Elma picked up a stack of books that were hidden under the material.

"Another woman, whom I've never met, was going to buy some books but changed her mind."

Elma handed the basket to Thelma. "Why don't you take this to the back room? After I put the fabric and books away, I'll meet you there."

Thelma was on the verge of telling her sister that putting those items away could wait until after they'd eaten, but Elma, being such a tidy person, would never rest until the counter was clean. "Okay," she responded. "I'll take everything out of the basket and set it on the table. We'll eat as soon as you get there."

LaGrange

"The weather isn't as warm as the last time we were here." Joseph grimaced as a chill ran down his back.

"It's a lot colder," Delbert agreed. "Glad it wasn't like this when we brought Elma and Thelma here. I'm sure Elma would have complained." He looked out over the pond. "I'm not even sure if the fish will bite today. They probably won't be hungry."

"Speaking of food, have you made any plans for Thanksgiving?" Joseph asked as he sat on a rock near the edge of the pond.

"Not yet, but that's still a few weeks away."

"True, but there's nothing like planning ahead."

Delbert chuckled. "So now you're into planning ahead, huh? Used to be that you just did things as they came along."

"People change." Joseph reached over and patted his dog's head. Ginger grunted and looked up at him with soulful brown eyes.

"What are your plans for Thanksgiving?" Delbert baited his hook.

"Mom's planning a dinner, and she said I could invite Thelma." Joseph grinned. When he'd told his parents about meeting Thelma and going out with her a few times, Mom had eagerly suggested he invite his new girlfriend to dinner, saying she and Dad would be anxious to meet her.

"What about Elma?" Delbert asked. "I doubt that Thelma would come without her twin sister."

"Of course Elma will be included. My invitation will

be to her, and you too."

Delbert popped a piece of gum into his mouth and starting chomping. "Am I supposed to be Elma's date?"

Joseph shrugged. "Only if you wanna be. It will be another opportunity for you to get to know her better."

"I guess you're right, but the way things have gone so far between us, I don't think there's much hope of us having a permanent relationship."

Joseph felt bad hearing that. Even though he hadn't known Thelma very long, he was convinced that he'd found the woman God intended him to have. He wished that was the case for his friend Delbert too.

Chapter 25

Topeka

"Sister, I don't feel so well." Clutching her stomach, Thelma sank to the couch.

Elma did the same. "I don't feel well either. I think we may be coming down with the flu that's been going around."

Thelma nodded slowly. "Given all the people we come in contact with at the store, we could have easily picked up the bug."

"What are your symptoms?" Elma asked.

"Besides my stomach doing flip-flops, my body aches, and I feel hot and sweaty."

"Same here. Unless we feel better than this in the morning, I don't see any way we can go to Mr. and Mrs. Beechy's house for the Thanksgiving meal."

Thelma leaned her head against the sofa and moaned. "As much as I was looking forward to going, we can't take the chance of exposing the others to whatever is plaguing us right now."

"Maybe you should let Joseph know we won't be there. Then we need to go to bed."

"You're right. If we don't show up, he's bound to be worried." Thelma forced herself to stand up then shuffled across the room. "I'll grab a flashlight and go out to the phone shack to make the call. I hope Joseph checks his messages in the morning."

Elma hated being sick, but she was actually glad they wouldn't be going to the Beechys' tomorrow for Thanksgiving. Truthfully, she would rather make dinner here, for just her and Thelma. As it was, it looked like the only thing they'd be eating was some hot chicken noodle soup—and that was only if they could keep it down.

As Elma pulled back the covers and crawled into bed, a shiver went through her. If she and Thelma were at home right now, Mom would be fussing over them, making sure they had plenty of liquids to keep them hydrated.

I wonder what Mom and Dad will be doing tomorrow. I'll bet they'll have a big Thanksgiving meal at one of Mom's sisters'. Or maybe Mom is cooking and some of the family will come to their house to eat.

Huddling under the blankets, tears moistened Elma's cheeks as she thought about all the delicious food she and Thelma had helped Mom prepare for past Thanksgiving meals. In addition to the turkey, there had been plenty of buttery mashed potatoes, tart cranberry sauce, and moist stuffing. She could almost see the steam rising from the brown glazed turkey as Dad carved thick slices for each of their plates.

As she drifted off to sleep, Elma said a silent prayer: *Heavenly Father, please bless Mom and Dad and those who will share a meal at their table tomorrow. Help Thelma and me to feel better. Guide and direct our lives, and give us wisdom in all matters.*

LaGrange

As Joseph left for his folks' the following morning, he thought about checking phone messages but decided it could wait until he got home. Since this was Thanksgiving, it was doubtful that anyone would call him anyway. He sure looked forward to eating dinner at his folks', but the best part was being able to introduce them to Thelma and her twin sister. He knew they would like her, and Elma too. *Sure wish Delbert had strong feelings for Elma, the way I do for Thelma,* he thought.

Over the last couple of weeks, he and Delbert had gone several more places with the girls, including a day of shopping that included lunch at the Blue Gate Restaurant. Each time they were together, Joseph felt a stronger connection to Thelma. He was almost sure that if things kept going this way, he would eventually ask her to marry him—if he could get up the nerve. He'd been doing better about not stuttering when he spoke to Thelma, but when it came to offering a marriage proposal, he would trip over his words so badly that she wouldn't even know what he said.

Delbert and I have been doing things together for a long time. It won't be the same if I get married and he doesn't. Joseph thumped his head. *Why am I even thinking such thoughts? I haven't been courting Thelma that long and don't really know how she feels about me.*

As Joseph's horse and buggy rounded the next bend, he made a decision. If he got the chance to speak with Thelma alone today, he would gather his courage and express how he felt about her. "Sure hope I don't lose my nerve."

"I'm glad you joined us today," Joseph's mother, Dora, said when Delbert entered their home.

He smiled, sniffing the air appreciatively. "I'm glad you invited me. Since I have no family living close by, I'd have probably been at home, eating alone. And I sure wouldn't have fixed a big Thanksgiving dinner."

She gave his arm a gentle squeeze. "You've been a good friend to Joseph, and we think of you as family."

"Speaking of Joseph, is he here yet? I didn't see his rig parked outside."

Dora motioned to the door leading to the living room. "He's in there with his daed. The reason you didn't see his buggy is because it's in the shed. Since my son will be spending the night, he figured he'd get the buggy out of the weather."

"That's a good idea," Delbert said. "I hear it's supposed to snow either tonight or tomorrow."

"You're welcome to spend the night too."

"That's nice of you, but I'll probably head for home sometime later this evening." Delbert moved across the room. "Guess I'll head into the other room and see what Joe's up to."

"Would you tell him and his daed that the turkey is almost done? We'll eat as soon as Elma and Thelma get here. I'm so glad you and Joseph have both found girlfriends. I'm looking forward to meeting them." A wide smile spread over Dora's freckled face. There was no doubt about it—Joseph had inherited his mother's red hair and fair complexion.

Delbert was tempted to tell Joseph's mother that Elma wasn't his girlfriend but saw no point in going into that right now. Instead, he excused himself and left the kitchen.

When Delbert entered the living room, he found Joseph and his father, Vern, visiting on the sofa. "Oh good, you're here." Joseph stood. "Did you see any sign of Elma and Thelma on the road?"

Delbert shook his head, taking a seat in the recliner across from them. "I'm surprised they aren't here already."

"Me too," Joseph agreed. "Sure hope they were able to follow my directions to Mom and Dad's house. It's not that hard to find, but if they took a wrong turn, they may be lost."

"You worry too much, son." Vern looked at Delbert and grinned. "It's good to see you."

Delbert smiled. "Same here."

Joseph pulled out his pocket watch to check the time.

"I'm wondering what we should do about dinner if the twins don't get here soon."

"Your mamm hasn't said it's time to eat yet, so I wouldn't worry about that." Delbert smiled. "Speaking of the twins, I'm glad we got their barn stained last week. With the snow that's predicted, if we hadn't done it then, it may have had to wait till spring."

"That's true," Joseph agreed. "But come spring, I think we ought to see about painting the house for them, don't you?" He stretched his legs.

Delbert nodded. "Their place is looking better and better."

"I was talking to Joe before you got here about those young women you two have been courting," Vern spoke up. "Told him I think it's nice that you both have girl-friends now." He scratched his balding head. "Makes me wonder which of you will get married first."

Joseph's ears turned pink. Delbert jumped up and moved closer to the fireplace. The last thing he wanted was to talk about marriage.

"All I've got to say," Vern continued, "is that it's about time."

Dora stepped into the room then and announced that the turkey was done. "Since your lady friends aren't here yet, I'll try to keep everything warm. But at some point we may have to eat without them." She brushed her hands on her apron. "If they arrive after we've already started eating, or even have finished the meal, there will be plenty of food left over to feed them."

Joseph stood and began to pace. "Thelma and Elma should have been here long before this. There's no way I can eat till they get here."

"Maybe they're not coming," Delbert said. "Could be that something came up to keep them at home."

"I can't imagine what it would be." Joseph moved over to stand beside Delbert. "If they weren't coming, I'm sure Thelma would have called."

"Does she have our phone number?" Dora asked.

"No, but she has mine, and—" Joseph stopped talking and grabbed his jacket and hat.

"Where are you going?" Dora called when Joseph was almost to the door.

"I didn't check my phone messages last night or this morning. I'm heading back to my house right now to see if there's any word from Thelma or her sister."

"Hold up," Delbert said, "I'll go with you. We can take my rig."

When Delbert pulled his horse and buggy next to Joseph's phone shack, Joseph hopped out and hurried inside. He flipped on the battery-operated light and took a seat. He was relieved when he found a message from Thelma but concerned when she said in a weak voice that she and her sister had come down with the flu and wouldn't be able to join them for Thanksgiving. He'd so wanted her to meet Mom and Dad.

Joseph picked up the receiver and dialed her number. When her answering machine came on, he left a message, saying if she needed anything to let him know and that he'd come by sometime tomorrow to check on them. Then he got back into Delbert's buggy. "The twins are *grank*. They have the flu and won't be coming to dinner. I'm really disappointed."

"Sorry to hear they're sick," Delbert said, "but there will be other times when you and Thelma can get together."

"I hope so." Joseph folded his arms and stared straight ahead, barely aware that a few snowflakes had begun falling. He had no appetite for food, but Mom had worked hard fixing the meal. So he'd force himself to eat a decent-sized portion and try not to worry about the twins.

As he and Delbert headed back to his parents' home, the road was quickly covered with a white film of crystals. What a beautiful night this would have been to go on a buggy ride with Thelma.

Chapter 26

Topeka

By Monday morning, the twins felt well enough to work in the store, although they were both still a little weak. Joseph had come by on Friday. He'd been nice enough to drop off a basket with leftovers from their Thanksgiving meal. After eating soup for three days, the leftovers she and Elma had heated for Sunday's meal tasted so good. Thelma had called and left a message for Joseph this morning, letting him know that she and Elma were fully recovered, and saying how much they'd enjoyed the food. She had been so disappointed that they'd missed Thanksgiving and the opportunity to meet Joseph's parents.

Pulling her thoughts back to the task at hand, Thelma glanced in the box she held and smiled as she waited for her sister to unlock the store. She and Elma had decided to bring the kittens to the store, hoping to give them away. It was getting to be a challenge going down to the basement with a basket of laundry and trying not to step on a kitten.

Thelma placed the box near the front door and went to straighten some bolts of material. As she worked, she reflected on her relationship with Joseph. The more time they spent together, the more she found herself falling in love with him. She continued to fantasize about what it would be like to be his wife and knew that should he ever ask her to marry him, her answer would be yes. Of course, that would depend on how things progressed with Elma and Delbert. So far, their relationship didn't seem to be going anywhere, but Thelma continued to hope things would get better.

They must feel something for each other, Thelma thought, *or they wouldn't keep double-dating with us.*

"Two of the busslin are gone."

Thelma jumped at the sound of her sister's voice. The last time she'd seen Elma, she'd been at the front counter, waiting on a customer. "Really? Who took them?"

"Mary Lambright. She wanted the kittens for Richard and Philip."

"I'm sure the boys will be happy about that." Thelma smiled. "Danki for letting me keep the little white bussli I named Snowball."

"I didn't *let* you, Sister. You made that decision yourself. I just went along with it." Elma reached for the same bolt of material Thelma had straightened.

"What are you going to do with that?" Thelma questioned, waiting for her sister to redo the roll of cloth.

"I'm taking it up front. Doris Miller is here, and she asked if we had any fabric this color."

"Okay. I'm almost done here, so if you need any help, let me know."

"I will."

When Elma walked away, Thelma went back to straightening the bolts. She'd finished the last one when Delbert showed up.

"I'm surprised to see you," she said. "Are you doing more work for us today?"

He shook his head. "I dropped by to—"

"Did Joseph come too?" Thelma hoped she didn't sound overly anxious.

"No, I'm alone." Delbert removed his hat. "Came by to invite you to the surprise birthday party I'm throwin' for Joe this Friday evening. I know he'd be disappointed if you weren't there."

Thelma smiled, resting her hand against her hip. "That sounds like fun. My sister and I would like to come.

Is there anything we can bring?"

Delbert rubbed his chin. "How about a salad?"

Thelma bobbed her head. "That shouldn't be a problem. I'll either make a fruit or potato salad. Or maybe we'll bring both. Would that be okay?"

Delbert shrugged. "Sure, that'd be fine." He shuffled his feet a few times. "Guess I'd better be on my way. I have a few stops I need to make here in Topeka before I head back to LaGrange."

"What time should we be there?" Thelma asked, following him to the front of the store.

"Six o'clock. Joe's supposed to show up at my house at six thirty. He thinks the two of us are going out to a restaurant to eat." Delbert put his hat back on his head. "His birthday's Saturday, so I don't think he'll catch on."

"But won't he see all the buggies parked in your yard when he gets to your house?"

"I don't think so. I'm asking everyone to park around back. Make sure you get to my place no later than six." He opened the door and paused.

"Okay. Elma and I will see you Friday evening then."

"If you see Joe between now and then, don't let the cat outta the bag. I want him to be surprised."

"I won't say a word."

When Delbert left, Thelma returned to the fabric aisle and stood there with a big grin. She could hardly wait to see Joseph again and planned to use the stocking cap she'd knitted him for Christmas as a birthday gift instead.

Elma came over. "You're wearing a huge smile. What's going on? I saw Delbert leave. What did I miss?"

"He came by to invite us to Joseph's surprise birthday party on Friday night." Thelma clasped her hands together.

"What did you tell him?"

"I said we'd be happy to attend, and I offered to bring two salads." Thelma tipped her head. "You do want to go, I hope, because I wouldn't feel right about going without you."

Elma smiled. "Of course I'll go. Joseph is my friend too."

LaGrange

"I wonder why they didn't have this party tomorrow afternoon," Elma said as she guided Pearl down the road leading to Delbert's house. "This time of the year, it gets dark early. It's not the safest time to be on the road with a buggy."

"I guess having it tonight was the only way they could surprise him," Thelma said. "Are you anxious to see Delbert?"

Elma clenched her teeth, ignoring her sister's question. She knew Delbert well enough to know they had no future together. She was fairly certain he felt that way too. One thing Elma knew was that her sister was smitten with Joseph. *Maybe she will end up marrying him. That would sure make our mamm happy. It would give her and Dad the hope of becoming grandparents.*

"I don't see any buggies," Elma commented as she directed Pearl up Delbert's driveway. "Could we be the first ones here?"

"I doubt it. Delbert said he was asking everyone to park their rigs around back." Thelma spoke with an air of excitement.

"Guess we'd better head there too."

When Thelma and Elma entered the house, Thelma saw several other people. Delbert made the introductions, and Thelma was pleased to finally meet Joseph's parents.

"I'm Joe's sister, Katie," a pretty young woman with auburn hair said, extending her hand to Elma. "You must be Thelma."

Elma shook her head and motioned to Thelma. "I'm Elma. She's Thelma."

Katie's cheeks darkened. "Ach, you two look so much alike. How does my brother tell you apart?"

Thelma snickered. "He's gotten us mixed up a couple

of times, but since he knows me better now, he can usually tell by talking to me."

"It's nice to meet you both." Katie gestured to the tall man by her side. "This is my husband, Abe, and the little girl he's holding is our two-year-old daughter, Amanda."

"She's so sweet." Thelma reached out and took the child's hand, noting how soft it was.

"Should we take our salads to the kitchen?" Elma asked, looking at Delbert.

He nodded. "Jah, that'd be good. You can put them in the refrigerator."

Thelma followed Elma to the kitchen, where Joseph's mother and his aunt Linda had gone. After they put their salads away, Thelma turned to Dora and asked, "Is there anything we can do to help?"

"I found a package of sweet tea in Delbert's cupboard," Dora replied. "There's a metal spoon and a pitcher on the counter."

Thelma opened the powdered mix and dumped it into the glass container. Then she went to the sink and filled it with water. "I want to thank you for sharing your Thanksgiving food with me and my sister. It sure tasted good when we were finally able to eat it."

"I'm glad you and Elma are over the flu. That can get pretty nasty." Dora smiled as she put some cheese and crackers on a platter.

As Thelma stirred the mixture, someone shouted from the living room that Joseph's horse and buggy had pulled in. Hurrying to finish the job, Thelma stirred so hard that a chunk of glass broke. Sticky sweet tea spilled out all over the table and dripped onto the floor. Some also splashed on her arm. "What have I done?"

"Let me help you." Elma stepped forward and helped Thelma clean up the mess, while Katie threw away the glass pitcher. Then they all rushed into the living room in time to see Joseph enter. "Surprise! Happy birthday!" everyone hollered.

Chapter 27

Joseph was surprised to see all these people in Delbert's house. He hardly knew what to say. He wasn't used to being the center of attention and knew his face and ears must be as red as his hair.

Delbert thumped Joseph's back and grinned. "Are you surprised, my friend?"

All Joseph could do was nod as his gaze traveled around the room. All his friends and family were there except his brother Eli, who lived in Ohio. Most importantly though, Thelma and her sister had come. He knew who Thelma was too for Elma had a small scar on her right elbow, which he caught sight of right away, since her arms were folded. The twins were wearing different-colored dresses as well—Thelma in dark blue and Elma in green.

"I—I never expected this," Joseph stammered, looking at Delbert. "I thought the two of us were going out to eat."

"We're gonna eat here." Delbert gestured to everyone. "They all want to help celebrate your *gebottsdaag*."

"But my birthday's not till tomorrow."

Delbert slung his arm over Joseph's shoulder. "I know that, Joe, but I figured you might have made plans to spend your birthday with your aldi."

Truth was, Joseph hadn't made any plans for his birthday. For that matter, he'd made no mention of it to Thelma. "Well, I. . .uh. . ."

"Sorry, friend. I didn't mean to embarrass you," Delbert said quietly. Then he turned to the crowd and said, "Now that our guest of honor is here, why don't we eat?"

"That sounds good to me." Joseph's father led the way to the table.

Joseph moved quickly across the room to where Thelma stood beside Katie. "I'm glad you're here. Would you sit beside me, Thelma?"

"I'm not Thelma," she said with a small laugh, pointing. "She's over there."

Joseph looked across the table and saw the woman he'd thought was Elma sitting beside his mother.

"I—I saw that small scar on her arm, and I thought..."

"What you saw was a tea stain on my sister's arm," Elma explained.

Joseph touched his hot cheeks. He felt like a dunce. On top of that, his eyes must be going bad. How could he have mistaken the sweet tea on Thelma's arm for a scar? Making his way to the opposite side of the table, he quickly took a seat on the other side of her.

She smiled and said, "Happy birthday, Joseph."

"Danki. Have you met my mamm?"

Thelma nodded. "I met both of your parents, as well as your sister and her family, after Elma and I got here." She smiled. "Your niece is so sweet."

And so are you. Joseph could only nod. He knew better than to blurt out his thoughts in front of everyone. He wasn't even sure he could say that privately to Thelma.

After their silent prayer, Joseph enjoyed visiting as he ate his meal. He was impressed with how well Thelma got along with his young niece. *She would make such a good mother,* he thought.

When the meal was over, Joseph's mother brought out a chocolate cake—his favorite. Then Joseph blushed even more when everyone sang "Happy Birthday." Afterward, his sister cut the cake while Delbert got out vanilla ice cream and several kinds of toppings. Following that,

Joseph received presents from some who had come to the party, as well as many birthday cards. His best gift was the stocking cap Thelma had knitted. With the weather turning colder now, he'd be able to wear it right away. Not only that, but it made him feel special, knowing she'd probably put a lot of time into making it.

While the guests mingled in the kitchen and living room, Joseph and Thelma remained at the table. Joseph didn't know where he got the courage, but so that no one else would see, he reached under the table and took hold of Thelma's warm hand. Holding his breath, he slowly turned and looked into her ocean-blue eyes. He was glad when she held his gaze, gently squeezing his fingers in return.

"Let's play a game of Ping-Pong," Delbert suggested. "We can play doubles. How's that sound, Joe?"

Joseph and Thelma jumped up, releasing each other's hands. "That sounds like fun." Joseph looked briefly at Thelma, noticing that her cheeks were a rosy pink. "Thelma and I can be on one side, and you and Elma on the other."

Delbert couldn't believe that every time the ball came his way, Elma reached over and smacked it. The only good part of having her as his partner was that he and Elma were winning. But it would be nice if he got the opportunity to hit the ball once in a while. To make matters worse, Thelma and Joseph didn't seem to be trying that hard to win. They spent more time talking to each other and less time paying attention to what was going on. There was no doubt about it—his friend Joe was in love.

When the twins said it was time to leave, Joseph put on his new cap and said that he would walk Thelma to the buggy. "I think it would be nice if you walked with Elma too," he whispered to Delbert.

Delbert went reluctantly. They walked across the yard, crunching their way through the fresh-fallen snow. A few days ago, the temperatures had dropped when another clipper system pushed through. Delbert slowed his pace, hoping Elma would do the same. "Can I speak with you for a few minutes?"

"Certainly. Can we talk while I hitch my horse to the buggy?"

"That would be fine. I'll help you with the chore." Delbert glanced over his shoulder and saw Joseph and Thelma disappear behind the back of the buggy. No doubt he too wanted to spend some time with his date alone— only for a different reason.

As they began their task, Delbert leaned closer to Elma and said quietly, "I've been thinking and praying about us."

"Oh?" With the moon's brightness, he could see her curious expression.

"Whenever we're together, there seems to be a lot of tension between us. Have you felt it too?" He looked straight into her eyes.

"Jah."

"I think we should stop seeing each other socially."

Elma let out a quick breath of air. "I'm actually quite relieved we are having this conversation. I agree. . .we can't take this relationship any further."

Delbert's shoulders relaxed. "We tried to make it work, and to be honest, toward the end, I was putting Joe's needs ahead of my own."

She tipped her head and looked at him quizzically. "What do you mean?"

"Joe needed to gain self-confidence with Thelma. As he often did in the past, Joe leaned on me for support."

"Were you only going out with me to please Joseph?"

"Not in the beginning, but as time went on and I realized that you and I aren't suited, I continued to double-date because it was what Joe wanted."

"I see." She lowered her gaze to the ground.

He touched her arm. "I hope you're not upset."

She lifted her head to look at him again. "No, I understand, because truthfully, I agreed to keep seeing you to make my sister happy."

"Guess that makes us even then, huh?"

She gave a nod. "Putting others ahead of ourselves is a wonderful act of love and friendship. But at times we need to think about our own needs too."

"I agree, and I'm glad we had this talk." Delbert felt like the weight of the world had been lifted from his shoulders.

Feeling suddenly unsure of himself, Joseph reached out and took Thelma's hand as they stood behind the sisters' buggy. "I had a lot of fun tonight, and I'm glad you could be here to help celebrate my birthday."

"I'm glad too. Except for splattering myself with tea, I had an enjoyable time."

Joseph's heart pounded as he took a step closer. "Y–you're a very special girl, and I–I'm in love with you." He wished he could quiet his racing heart and speak without stumbling over his words.

"I love you too, Joseph." Thelma's voice was soft, and he stood staring at her beautiful face illuminated by the light of the moon. Then gathering his courage, Joseph drew Thelma into his arms and kissed her sweet lips. He was glad when she responded by kissing him back. Oh, what he wouldn't give to hold her like this every night for the rest of his life. But it was too soon to speak of marriage. Or was it?

"The horse is hitched, and we're ready to go, Sister," Elma called, interrupting the joy of the moment.

"All right, I'm coming." Thelma stared up at Joseph. "I guess it's time for us to go."

"I'll call or come by soon," Joseph said, walking her to the passenger's side of the buggy.

She smiled. "I'd like that."

As the twins drove away, Joseph waved until they

were out of sight. "Say, I have an idea," he said as he and Delbert walked back to the house. "Why don't we invite the twins to join us for supper tomorrow evening? Since that's my actual birthday, it would be nice if the four of us could spend it together, don't you think?"

Delbert stopped walking and turned to face Joseph. "Umm. . .there's something you should know."

"What's that?"

"I won't be seeing Elma socially anymore. Before you say anything else, you need to know that it was a mutual decision. Elma and I discussed it while we were hitching her horse to the buggy."

Joseph was disappointed to hear this. He'd really hoped Delbert and Elma would work things out. He wondered if his friend was being too picky, looking for little things he didn't like about Elma so he wouldn't have to give up his freedom. What was so great about living by himself anyway? Wouldn't Delbert be happier if he had a wife and children? Maybe not. Perhaps it wasn't meant for Delbert to be married.

"I feel so excited," Thelma said as she and Elma baked a batch of ginger cookies the following evening.

"What are you excited about?" Elma removed a cookie sheet from the oven.

Thelma pointed to the kitchen window. "Look at all that snow out there. It's so beautiful—just perfect for a sleigh ride."

Elma smiled. "Do you think we should get that old sleigh of Grandpa's out of the barn and let Pearl take us for a ride?"

Thelma drew in her lower lip. "It may be better to take Rusty, since he has more stamina than Pearl. And you know, since I've been working with him, he's better behaved."

Elma placed the cookies on a cooling rack. "I suppose it'll be okay to take Rusty, as long as you're driving."

"I was thinking of inviting Joseph and Delbert to join us. I'm sure one of them would be willing to sit in the driver's seat."

Elma frowned. "I thought it would just be the two of us."

"I think it would be more fun if the four of us went. Wouldn't you enjoy a romantic sleigh ride with Delbert?"

Elma sighed and sank into a chair at the table. "There's something I need to tell you, Sister."

"What's that?" Thelma sat too.

"After praying about it, I made a decision concerning Delbert." Elma brushed a splotch of flour from her apron. "We're not suited. I won't be going out with him anymore."

Thelma's heart gave a lurch. "Are you sure? I mean, won't you give it a little more time?"

Elma shook her head. "I've been with Delbert enough times to know that he's not the man God has for me."

Thelma realized now it had been wishful thinking on her part. If Elma had prayed about this, then it must not be God's will for her to be with Delbert. *Guess I won't be seeing Joseph anymore either.* Thelma's throat constricted. *It wouldn't be fair to break my promise and leave Elma all alone. But, oh, I will surely miss him.*

If she lived to be one hundred, Thelma would never forget the gentle touch of his lips against hers as they'd stood at the back of the buggy. She touched Elma's arm. "I guess the four of us won't be going for a romantic sleigh ride, after all."

"You and Joseph can still go. It can be a romantic evening for the two of you."

Thelma pushed away from the table and stood. "I think we ought to get the rest of these *kichlin* baked." Anything to keep from thinking about Joseph.

Chapter 28

"Y ou have a message from Joseph," Elma told Thelma when she came into the house the following Friday morning, after going to the phone shack.

Thelma turned from the sink where she'd been washing dishes. "What did he say?"

"Said he wanted to take you out to supper this evening, and he wondered why you haven't returned any of his calls this week." Elma removed her shawl and draped it over the back of a chair. "I'd like to know that too."

Thelma shrugged. "We've been busy at the store. With Christmas a couple of weeks away, people have been coming in to buy gifts and other things."

"I know we've been busy, but not so much that it would keep you from returning Joseph's calls."

Thelma reached for a wet glass to dry.

"There's a lot of snow on the ground, and it looks so beautiful. Wouldn't you enjoy going on a sleigh ride with Joseph?"

Putting the dried glass away, Thelma merely shrugged.

Elma moved over to the sink. "Are you avoiding Joseph? Has he said or done something to upset you, Sister?"

"Not really. I don't think things are going to work for him and me though."

"Why not?"

"We're two very different people. He's kind of quiet, and I'm always talking." Thelma grabbed a cup from the dish rack and continued her work.

"That shouldn't prevent you from having a relationship. Look at Mom and Dad. Their personalities are different, but they have a good marriage. Haven't you ever heard the expression 'Opposites attract'?"

Thelma set the cup on the counter. "Sure, but it doesn't work for everybody. Look at you and Delbert."

"It was different for us. It wasn't just our different personalities. We grated on each other's nerves." Elma put her hand on Thelma's arm. "Are you going to return Joseph's call?"

Feeling as if she were backed into a corner, Thelma nodded. "I'll go out to the phone shack and do it now."

As Thelma crunched her way through the snow, she tried to figure out what message to leave for Joseph. Should she come right out and say she didn't want to see him anymore, or would it be best to make up some excuse?

Thelma stepped into the phone shack. The fluttering in her stomach didn't help as she dialed Joseph's number. When his voice mail picked up she said: "Hello, Joseph, this is Thelma. I'm sorry for not returning your calls. We've been busy at the store this week." She paused and moistened her chapped lips with the tip of her tongue, struggling for words that wouldn't be a lie. "I—I appreciate the invitation to have supper with you, but I won't be able to go anywhere this evening. I hope you have a blessed Christmas with your family."

When Thelma hung up the phone, tears sprang to her eyes. Giving up her relationship with Joseph was one of the hardest things she'd ever done. Sometimes though, sacrifices needed to be made for the benefit of someone else, and this was one of those times.

"Are you sure you can manage on your own for a while?" Thelma asked around noon when she and Elma were working in the store.

Elma nodded. "I'll be fine. One of us needs to get to the post office and mail Mom and Dad's Christmas package."

Thelma's shoulders drooped. "I feel bad that they probably aren't coming here to celebrate with us, after all. It'll be a lonely day without them."

"I agree, and I'll miss them too. But this time of the year, the weather can change people's plans. The area around Sullivan is getting hit with cold weather right now. Mom said in her last message that a lot of snow has fallen there already and more is expected between now and Christmas." Elma tried to sound cheerful for her sister's sake, but the thought of spending Christmas without their folks made her feel sad too. Thanksgiving was bad enough, since it was the first holiday away from their parents, but now she'd have to find a way to get through Christmas too.

Thelma sighed. "Snow is pretty, but sometimes I wish our winters were warm like they are in Florida."

"Say, I have an idea." Elma placed her hand on Thelma's shoulder. "Why don't you invite Joseph to join us for Christmas dinner?"

Thelma looked toward the pile of mail that also needed to be taken to the post office. "I'm sure he's made plans to be with his family that day."

"Has he asked you to join them?"

"No, and even if he had, I wouldn't go." She dropped her gaze to the floor.

"Why not, for goodness' sake?"

"I wouldn't think of leaving you home by yourself on Christmas Day." Thelma slipped into her coat, gathered up the mail, and started for the door.

"Wait a minute," Elma called. "You forgot something." She held up her sister's black outer bonnet.

Thelma came back and got it. "Danki. I'll try not to be gone too long."

"Hold on. Don't forget this." Elma held up the package they were mailing to Mom and Dad.

"Oops. Not sure where my mind is today. Guess I left it in the bed this morning." Thelma shrugged her shoulders as she tucked the package under her arm.

"Be careful out there. The roads may be icy," Elma called, watching Thelma go out the door.

Something is not right with my sister, Elma thought as she grabbed the bottle of spray cleaner and a towel to wipe down the front counter.

No one else was in the store. The only noise Elma heard was the crackling of wood from the small woodstove. Elma relished this time of solitude when she could be by herself to reflect on all the good things the Lord had done for her and Thelma. *I'm beginning to see why Grandma and Grandpa left us their home and store. They wanted to teach us to be responsible and make it on our own. Of course someday, if Thelma marries Joseph, I will be living by myself, and I'll have more solitude than I know what to do with.*

The thought of living alone frightened her a bit, since she'd always had Thelma with her, but Elma had always known that someday one of them would fall in love, get married, and move away. She wasn't totally prepared for that yet. In her heart she'd always hoped that she and her twin would find their one true love at the same time. She knew it was a silly dream. Simply because she and Thelma were twins didn't mean they had to do everything exactly alike or at the same time. God had created them to be two individuals, and if they didn't begin a life of their own with a man they loved, they'd stay like they were now—two old-maid sisters always hoping for the love of a man. Or worse yet, blaming one or the other, years down the road, because it had never happened.

Elma's musings were interrupted when she heard the front door open, followed by the sound of heavy footsteps. She looked up and was surprised to see Joseph wearing the stocking cap Thelma had made him.

"I got your message, and I'd like to know what's going on," he said, stepping up to the counter.

Elma's forehead wrinkled. "What message?"

"Are you really too busy to go out with me, or have I done something wrong?" Joseph put both hands on the counter.

Elma's eyes widened. "Oh Joseph, you've got the wrong twin. I'm Elma."

Red blotches erupted on Joseph's cheeks. "Oh great. I've done it again." He glanced around. "Is Thelma here? I need to talk to her."

Elma shook her head. "She went to the post office awhile ago."

"When will she be back?" He sounded desperate.

"I'm not sure. But would you mind telling me what my sister's message said?"

"She said she's been too busy to call me all week and that she's not able to go out to supper with me tonight." He paused and pulled his cap down over his ears. "Have I done something to offend her? Has she said anything to you?"

"No, not really, but I have my suspicions."

"What does that mean?"

Elma leaned forward. "Listen, Joe, my sister and I will be hosting a Christmas caroling party with some of the young people in our district next Friday evening. I'd like you to be there."

"Are—are you sure?" Joseph stammered. "What if my being there upsets Thelma?"

"It won't. Trust me." Elma gave him what she hoped was a reassuring smile. "Everything is going to work out for the best."

Chapter 29

LaGrange

More snow had fallen in the area, and Joseph wondered if the caroling party was still on. He assumed it was, because he'd checked his messages before hitching his horse to the buggy, and the only one was from a customer, asking if his harness was done.

Joseph looked forward to this evening and being with Thelma. It would be the first time he'd been with her when Delbert wasn't around. He still felt bad that things hadn't worked out between Delbert and Elma. He'd really hoped his friend would find a wife and settle down, but maybe Delbert was too set in his ways.

As Joseph's rig drew closer to Topeka, his hands began to sweat. *What if Thelma isn't happy to see me? I hope Elma told her I was coming.*

Topeka

"Herschel Miller is here with his large open wagon and two draft horses," Thelma announced when she looked out the kitchen window and saw him coming up the driveway.

Elma joined her at the window. "It was nice of him to do that, because there wouldn't have been room for all of us to go caroling in Grandpa's sleigh."

"You're right about that. Guess we ought to take the sleigh out by ourselves sometime this winter though." Thelma sighed. She'd been looking forward to doing that with Joseph. *Stop thinking about him,* she chided herself.

Focus on the fun we're going to have this evening. She drew a sad face on the moisture collected on the pane of glass then quickly wiped it off, drying the rest of the window with a piece of cloth.

Thelma looked at Elma, hoping she hadn't noticed, and at the same time they said, "We'd best get ready."

Elma laughed. "We still need to get our coats, outer bonnets, gloves, and boots."

"Let's do that right now." Thelma followed Elma into the utility room, and once they'd gotten their things, they returned to the kitchen to make sure everything was ready.

"I think we have everything ready for our refreshment time after we get back from caroling." Cookies, pretzels, and popcorn were set out on the table. They would also build a bonfire and roast hot dogs.

"Do you know how many are coming?" Thelma asked.

"I think there will be twenty of us."

Thelma smiled. "A nice big group to sing the Christmas songs we all know and love. I hope the places we stop by will enjoy hearing the music."

"I'm sure they will, Sister. Whenever we went caroling back home, everyone we sang to seemed to appreciate it."

A knock sounded on the door, and Thelma went to open it. Herschel greeted her with a friendly smile. "I'm glad you two are doing this for our *younga*," he said. "It's a perfect night for a caroling party."

"We're happy to do it." Thelma opened the door wider. "Why don't you come inside until everyone gets here? There's hot coffee on the stove."

"That sounds nice." Herschel sat down after she handed him a cup of coffee. "Danki."

The three of them visited around the kitchen table until the young people showed up. Then Thelma and Elma put on their outer garments and followed Herschel outside.

Soon everyone climbed onto the back of the wagon and took seats on bales of straw. Thelma was about to get on when she spotted another horse and buggy pulling in.

"I thought everyone was here," she said, looking at Elma.

A few seconds later, Joseph got out and tied his horse to the hitching rail. "What's he doing here, Sister? Did you know he was coming?"

Elma nodded and lowered her voice. "He stopped by the store last week, and I invited him to join us this evening."

"Don't you think you should have said something to me about that?" Thelma couldn't imagine why Elma would invite Joseph to the caroling party and not tell her.

Elma slipped her arm around Thelma's waist and gave her a squeeze. "Relax, and enjoy the evening."

Thelma shivered and pulled her coat tighter around her neck. *How can I relax with Joseph heading toward me?*

"Thelma?" Joseph asked, stepping up to the woman he believed was his girlfriend.

"Jah, it's me. Did you think I was Elma?"

"No. Yes." He pulled his knitted cap over his ears, knowing they must be pink. "Well, I wasn't sure. When I came by the store last week I—I thought she was you." *Don't start stuttering now, Joseph.* He reached out and touched her arm. "It's good to see you, Thelma. I've been looking forward to tonight ever since Elma invited me to go caroling with you."

"Speaking of caroling, we'd better get on the wagon before they take off without us."

Joseph grinned. "Let's go!" He hopped up and reached his hand out to Thelma, helping her onto the wagon as well. He patted the seat beside him. When she joined him on the bale of straw, he noticed that she didn't seem like her usual cheerful self. He couldn't put his finger on it, but thinking it would be best not to say anything in front of everyone, he let it go. "Here, you may need this as we begin moving down the road." Joseph placed a blanket across Thelma's lap.

She offered him a smile and seemed to relax a bit. "You're welcome to share it with me."

Joseph pulled part of the blanket over his knees, and a few minutes later they were on their way.

The joyful group laughed, visited, and sang as they traveled the roads, taking them through downtown Topeka and onto several of the back roads. They stopped by some church members' homes, serenading them with Christmas songs. Joseph was having a good time, and Thelma seemed to be as well. At one point, she'd even leaned close to him and said, "You have a nice singing voice, Joe."

He smiled. "I enjoy singing Christmas songs." *Especially when I'm with you,* he added silently. Joseph thought the chilly winter's night was perfect weather for Christmas caroling.

"Look over there." Joseph pointed at a curious raccoon watching them pass before disappearing behind some bushes.

Thelma sighed. "It's a beautiful night."

Nothing is as beautiful as you, Joseph thought, wishing he could say it out loud. Right now, he would give anything to be alone with Thelma.

When their driver announced that the next place would be their last stop, Joseph felt disappointed. He didn't want the evening to end. He hoped before he left that he could talk privately with Thelma.

Elma asked if everyone was hungry and said when they returned to her and Thelma's house, they'd build a bonfire and roast hot dogs. Joseph was happy about that. Not because he was hungry, but because it would give him more time with Thelma. It was strange how she was acting tonight—one minute quiet and aloof—the next minute laughing.

"It doesn't look like anyone is home here," one of the young men shouted. "See, there's no light in any of the windows."

"Look, there's a katz!" Thelma pointed to the cat sitting on the front porch. The feline's gray coat was illuminated by the light of the silvery moon.

"Should we sing to the katz?" someone shouted.

"Why not?" another person responded.

Everyone began singing, "We wish you a blessed Christmas. . . We wish you a blessed Christmas. . . We wish you a blessed Christmas and a joyous New Year!"

The front door opened, and an elderly Amish man with a cane stepped out, holding a flashlight. Joseph didn't recognize him, but then he didn't know that many people living in Topeka.

To Joseph's surprise, the man stepped off his porch and started singing to the carolers. His cat came over to him and rubbed against his leg. Thelma laughed and joined him in song. Soon, the others accompanied them as well. Joseph could hardly wait to see what the rest of the night would bring.

Chapter 30

Although Thelma enjoyed being with Joseph, she knew she couldn't count on more evenings like this. Before the night was over, she would have to tell Joseph that she couldn't see him again. He may not understand if she tried to explain that unless her sister was being courted by a man, there was no way she could keep seeing him. Most people did not understand the bond identical twins had.

Thelma tried not to think about it as the lively group sang their way back to her and Elma's house. But the closer they got, the more apprehensive she felt. By the time Herschel guided his team up their driveway, Thelma had broken out in a cold sweat. Clutching the scarf around her neck didn't seem to help the chill that went straight to her bones. *I should have told Joseph that I couldn't see him anymore when I left him a message last week. That would have been easier than saying it to his face.*

She thought once again about the kiss they'd shared after Joseph's birthday party, and wished now she hadn't let it happen. If she'd only known then that Elma wouldn't be seeing Delbert anymore, she would have ended it with Joseph that night. There was no point in thinking about that now. She needed to get through this evening without breaking down.

When the wagon came to a stop, Joseph hopped down and extended his hand to Thelma. Once she was on the ground, he put his hand gently behind her back as they walked through the yard.

"Would you like me to get a fire started?" Joseph asked Thelma.

She nodded. "That would be nice."

"Would you like to help me with that?" he questioned.

She swallowed hard, barely able to look at him. "I need to go inside and help Elma get the hot dogs and other things out. I'm sure some of the young men will help you gather wood for the fire."

Joseph gave her a heart-melting smile and headed across the yard to a group of young men who had starting making snowballs. "No snowball games tonight," he called. "We need to get a fire going so we can eat."

As the evening wore on, Thelma grew quieter. She could barely eat her hot dog, much less enjoy any of the cookies. All she could think about was how attentive Joseph was being and how much she dreaded telling him good-bye. At least he wasn't part of their church district and she wouldn't have to see him every other Sunday. That would have made things even more difficult.

"You've been awfully quiet since we got back from caroling," Joseph said, interrupting Thelma's thoughts. "Are you feeling all right?"

"I'm fine. Just tired is all."

"It looks like things are winding down now and most of the young people are going home." Joseph touched her arm. "If it's okay, I'd like to stay until everyone is gone so we can talk."

"That's fine. I'd like to speak with you as well."

Half an hour later, everyone had gone and Thelma began to gather the paper plates and other things left over from the meal they'd shared around the bonfire.

"Don't worry about that, Sister," Elma said. "I'll take care of cleaning up. Sit and enjoy the last of the glowing embers with Joseph." Elma scooped everything into a wicker basket and hurried inside before Thelma could formulate a response. She wondered if her sister knew what she was about to tell Joseph and wanted to give her time to do it. Quite often when either Thelma or Elma planned to do something, the other twin had a feeling about it—almost as though they could read each other's minds.

Joseph moved his folding chair closer to Thelma's. "There's something I want to say," he said, taking her hand.

"I—I need to tell you something too," she murmured. "But you can go first."

Joseph cleared his throat a couple of times. "We've only known each other a few months, and it's probably too soon to be talking about marriage, but—"

"Joseph, things are not going to work out for us. After tonight, I won't be able to see you again."

"Why, Thelma? You said you loved me the other night. And you let me kiss you."

Tears sprang to her eyes. "You may not understand, but I can't have a relationship with you when my sister has no one."

"You're right, I don't understand. I love you, Thelma, and I think God brought us together."

"I love you too, but Elma and I have a special bond. When we were little girls we talked about what it would be like when we fell in love and got married." Thelma paused and swiped at the tears rolling down her cheeks. "We promised each other that until we both found the right man, neither of us would get married."

"Are you saying that you won't marry me unless Elma falls in love with a man and they make plans to be married?" The wrinkles across Joseph's forehead revealed his confusion.

Thelma nodded slowly. "But that may never happen, and you need to be free to find the right woman, so—"

"He already has, and you, Thelma, are being ridiculous!"

Thelma whirled around, surprised to see her sister standing behind her, hands on both hips. "You. . .you startled me, Elma. I thought you were in the house."

"I was, but I remembered that I'd left my gloves lying on the log. So I came back out to get them." Elma moved around to stand in front of Thelma. Then she leaned down and looked directly at her. "That was a silly promise we made to each other when we were kinner, and I won't allow you to sacrifice the love you have found with Joseph when it's completely unnecessary." She paused, placing her hands on Thelma's shoulders. "I was perfectly happy before I met Delbert, and I will be fine on my own. In fact, you and Joseph have my blessing. I would be miserable if I were the cause of you two breaking up."

Thelma didn't know what to say. Could she really marry Joseph and leave her sister alone? Would that even be fair?

Elma gestured to Joseph, asking them both to stand. Then she took Thelma's hand and placed it in Joseph's. "You two make a good couple. I truly believe you belong together. Now, I'm going to get my gloves and leave you alone to work things out." She smiled, grabbed her gloves, and went back to the house.

Joseph turned to face Thelma. "What do you have to say about that?"

She smiled through her tears. "I've always tried to please my sister, and if she really wants us to keep courting, then I guess I can't argue with that."

Joseph bent his head and captured her lips in a sweet, gentle kiss. "And to think, we never would have met if you hadn't made that crazy-looking lopsided cake. I believe this is going to be my best Christmas yet. By next year at this time, I hope we can be married."

"I know this will be a good Christmas too." Thelma's smile widened. "I love you, Joseph."

Filled with such happiness as she'd never felt before,

Thelma barely noticed how the moon encased them in its brilliant light. All she felt was the warmth of Joseph's arms holding her close as she leaned her head against his chest. *And maybe,* she thought, *by next year, my sister will have found the man of her dreams too.*

Epilogue

The next October

As Thelma sat quietly beside Joseph at their bride-and-groom's corner table, she thought about the changes that had occurred over the past year. Most important was that her and Joseph's hearts and lives were now joined through the love of God. Not only had she and Joseph been married this morning, with both of their families present, but tomorrow they would be moving into the house across the street from Elma. Joseph had recently sold his business in LaGrange and purchased the harness shop in Topeka, since the previous owner was ready to retire.

"What a glorious day this has been," Thelma whispered to Joseph.

"Jah. Even our wedding cake is perfect for us," he joked, pointing to the lopsided cake sitting before them.

She laughed. "This time it's Elma's fault. She said the cake batter didn't rise evenly, but I have to wonder if she made it this way on purpose to remind us of how we first met."

"You could be right. And speaking of Elma. . ." Joseph gestured to the table where Thelma's twin sister sat. "Who's that man she's talking to?"

"Oh, you mean the one sitting between her and Delbert?"

"Jah, I don't recognize him."

"That's Delbert's cousin, Myron Bontrager. He's visiting Delbert, so that's why he's here."

Joseph's eyebrows scrunched together. "I've heard Dell mention his cousin once or twice, saying that he too is a bachelor, but this is the only time I've ever seen him. From what I understand, he lives in southern Indiana. I wonder if this is his first visit to the area."

Thelma shook her head. "No, it's not. When Delbert introduced Myron to me awhile ago, he said he'd been here last October."

"Really? Dell never mentioned that."

"And here's the surprising part."

Joseph leaned closer.

"Myron is the other person who was bidding on our lopsided Christmas cake at the cooking show."

"What?" Joseph's eyes widened.

"It's true. When Myron saw our lopsided wedding cake today, he admitted he was the bidder and said he'd only wanted the cake so he could meet me and Elma." Thelma smiled, watching her sister and Myron in deep conversation. "When Myron realized it was his own cousin he'd been bidding against, he finally gave up and let Delbert win. Delbert didn't know Myron was there that day until he confessed it to him later on."

"I'm glad he let Delbert win." Looking lovingly at Thelma, Joseph added, "I wonder if there's a chance that your sister and Dell's cousin could get together. They're both smiling pretty good right now."

Thelma reached under the table and took hold of her groom's hand. "Now wouldn't it be something if our lopsided cake brought another couple together?"

Grandma's Christmas Cake

Ingredients:

3 cups sifted cake flour

2½ teaspoons baking
powder

½ teaspoon salt

1¾ cups sugar

⅔ cup butter

2 eggs

1½ teaspoons vanilla

1¼ cups milk

1 small (3 ounce) box
red Jell-O

1 small (3 ounce) box
green Jell-O

1 (8 ounce) tub Cool
Whip

Preheat oven to 350 degrees. Sift flour, baking powder, and salt together in bowl and set aside. In mixing bowl, cream sugar and butter. Add eggs and vanilla. Beat until fluffy, scraping down sides of bowl frequently. Slowly beat in flour mixture alternately with milk. Mix batter thoroughly and pour into two greased and floured 9-inch round pans.

Bake for 30 to 35 minutes or until done. Cool. Prick cakes several times with fork and leave in pans. Dissolve red Jell-O in 1 cup boiling water and carefully pour over one cake. Dissolve green Jell-O in 1 cup boiling water and pour over other cake. Refrigerate overnight or for a few hours.

Take cakes out of pans using spatula and put on plate, one on top of the other, spreading filling between layers (see recipe below). Frost cake with 1 tub Cool Whip. Decorate with red and green sprinkles if desired.

Filling:

1 (8 ounce) package
cream cheese, softened

1 (8 ounce) tub Cool
Whip

In bowl, mix cream cheese and Cool Whip until thoroughly combined.

New York Times, award-winning author **Wanda E. Brunstetter** is one of the founders of the Amish fiction genre. Wanda's ancestors were part of the Anabaptist faith, and her novels are based on personal research intended to accurately portray the Amish way of life. Her books are well-read and trusted by many Amish, who credit her for giving readers a deeper understanding of the people and their customs. When Wanda visits her Amish friends, she finds herself drawn to their peaceful lifestyle, sincerity, and close family ties.

Wanda enjoys photography, ventriloquism, gardening, bird-watching, beachcombing, and spending time with her family. She and her husband Richard have been blessed with two grown children, six grandchildren, and two great-grandchildren.

To learn more about Wanda, visit her website at www.wandabrunstetter.com.

Jean Brunstetter became fascinated with the Amish when she first went to Pennsylvania to visit her father-in-law's family. Since that time, Jean has become friends with several Amish families and enjoys writing about their way of life. She also likes to put some of the simple practices followed by the Amish into her daily routine. Jean lives in Washington State with her husband, Richard Jr. and their three children, but takes every opportunity to visit Amish communities in several states. In addition to writing, Jean enjoys boating, gardening, and spending time on the beach. Visit Jean's website at www.jeanbrunstetter.com.

Enjoy More Christmas from Wanda E. Brunstetter!

A Christmas Prayer

Only the brave—or foolhardy—would attempt a cross-country journey late in the season. Three wagons meet up in Independence, Missouri, in April 1850, and their owners decide to keep forging ahead despite many setbacks and delays. December finds them in the Sierra Nevada Mountains when a sudden snowstorm traps them, obscuring the trail. Cynthia Cooper is traveling with her mother and the man she has promised to marry. But as Christmas is upon them and they are hunkered down in a small cabin, she is forced to reevaluate her reasons for planning to marry fellow-traveler Walter Prentice. When a widowed father heading to a California ranch and a gold prospector both show an interest in Cynthia, she weighs her dreams for marriage alongside her responsibility to care for her mother. Can love win over her timid heart?

Paperback / 978-1-68322-657-4 / $12.99